there
will
come
a
time

Carrie Arcos

Simon Pulse   New York   London   Toronto   Sydney   New Delhi

This book is a work of fiction. Any references to historical events,
real people, or real places are used fictitiously. Other names, characters, places,
and events are products of the author's imagination, and any resemblance to
actual events or places or persons, living or dead, is entirely coincidental.

SIMON PULSE

An imprint of Simon & Schuster Children's Publishing Division
1230 Avenue of the Americas, New York, NY 10020
First Simon Pulse hardcover edition April 2014
Text copyright © 2014 by Carrie Arcos
Jacket photograph copyright © 2014 by Jamo Saren/Arcangel Images
All rights reserved, including the right of reproduction
in whole or in part in any form.
SIMON PULSE and colophon are registered
trademarks of Simon & Schuster, Inc.
For information about special discounts for bulk purchases,
please contact Simon & Schuster Special Sales at 1-866-506-1949
or business@simonandschuster.com.
The Simon & Schuster Speakers Bureau can bring authors to your
live event. For more information or to book an event contact the
Simon & Schuster Speakers Bureau at 1-866-248-3049 or visit our website
at www.simonspeakers.com.
Book design by Regina Flath
The text of this book was set in Adobe Caslon Pro.
Manufactured in the United States of America
2 4 6 8 10 9 7 5 3 1
Full CIP data is available from the Library of Congress.
ISBN 978-1-4424-9585-2
ISBN 978-1-4424-9587-6 (eBook)

One

When Chris speaks, his hands flop around like dying fish on the deck of a ship. I try not to stare, but it's impossible. They're pale, scaly things, too small for his wrists, more like the hands of a kid than a man. He's going on and on about how much progress he thinks we've made, about how I'm on my way toward health. I notice that he doesn't say I'm healed. Everyone is always in recovery. No one is ever whole. I didn't need six therapy sessions to tell me that I'll never be whole again.

"Mark, so what do you think?"

Hearing my name, I lift my gaze and meet his eyes. "What?"

"How have these sessions been for you?"

I'm unsure how to respond. If I say they've been helpful, then it's as if I'm admitting that he's been right—that everyone's been right—and I've needed counseling. If I say they haven't, he'll write something like, *Needs more time,* and then I'll have to waste additional hours of my life with this guy and his stupid fish hands.

I take a different approach. "It's always good to talk things out." Not that I've done any talking. I've basically repeated Chris's phrases back to him, telling him what I think he wants to hear. It's easy, especially with adults who think listening means nodding and taking notes and making assumptions. Assumptions like Chris made when we met. He took one look at me—male, Filipino, teen, beanie, white plugs, red T-shirt, jeans—and said, "What's up?" as if he was excited to practice his teen vernacular. I held out my hand and said, "Pleased to meet you." I didn't want to be there, but I'd been raised to respect authority. My formality must have thrown him, because he gave a thin smile after shaking my hand and motioned for me to sit in the black leather chair facing his desk.

Chris's brown eyes perk up at my response. I've probably made his day.

"Yes, yes, it is, Mark. I'm glad you can see that." He folds his tiny hands on the desk in front of him. "I hope you'll take the tools you've learned here and apply them with your family, your friends. Know that you're not alone. I am always here if you need to talk."

I nod. Sure, at 110 bucks an hour.

"Great." Chris gets up, signaling that our session is done. "Can you send your father in on your way out?"

In the waiting room, Dad stands in front of a painting of an ocean.

"Um, Chris wants you," I say.

Dad glances at my eyes, then looks at the floor as he says, "Okay." He pats my shoulder twice as he walks by, and closes the door to Chris's office behind him.

I stand in his place across from the picture. The sea is dark blue and streams of sunlight break through a patch in the clouds, illuminating the water, making it sparkle. A couple of birds fly across the horizon. A lighthouse sits atop a cliff directing a beam of light at a small sailboat in the corner of the canvas. The caption underneath reads: AFTER THE STORM.

They say grief is an ocean measured in waves and currents, rocking and tossing you about like a boat stranded in the middle of the deep. But this is not true. Grief is a dull blade against the skin of your soul. It takes its time doing its work. Grief will slowly drive you crazy, until you try to sever yourself like some kind of wounded animal caught in a trap. You'd rather maim yourself and be free.

But you'll never be free because you'll always remember. I remember. I remember my twin sister, Grace. So I press up against the blade even harder.

Two

Everyone is going to die.

You could wake up, get out of bed, trip over a pair of sneakers on the way to the bathroom, fall down the stairs, and break your neck. You could get some crazy disease. You could cross the street and get hit by a car. You could have a brain aneurysm, or maybe choke on a piece of hot dog like Jimmy Trevino did during lunch freshman year. While most of us were standing there with our mouths open, thinking, *Do something!* Miles crashed through the tables and chairs, grabbed Jimmy around the middle, and jammed his fists up under Jimmy's rib cage until the small piece of meat shot out of Jimmy's mouth. Jimmy lived, but another minute and he could have been brain-dead, which is pretty much like being dead, or he could have been dead-dead.

The point is you die. Most of the time you don't see it coming.

I used to cover my head with a black hoodie thinking it'd help me be invisible. But a seventeen-year-old male walking the streets alone in a hoodie automatically invites suspicion. I swear it's why I was questioned once by an officer. I gave him some story about how I was on my way home, and he let me off with a warning. Sometimes I wear a baseball cap. The front hangs over my face like a duck's bill, casting a shadow I try to hide in.

Tonight's been uneventful. I walked underneath the bridge where the LA river trickles into the cement arroyo, steering clear of the narrow path that curves up alongside the back part of the bridge. I made the mistake of going that way a couple of months ago and ran into a homeless man and his knife. To be fair, it was the middle of the night and I probably scared the guy. I didn't stick around to find out.

When I step onto the bridge, it narrows in front of me like a tunnel. The usual dizziness comes, what I guess is vertigo, along with the bile. I resist the urge to throw up. Taking deep breaths, I close my eyes and practice one of Chris's meditation techniques that has actually proved useful. I simply relax and don't stop any image or thought from entering my mind.

I'm back in the car. Grace is next to me. She's singing along to the radio, like she always does. Her voice is a deep alto. We're going . . . where are we going again? The movies? I can't remember.

The tall lampposts, each lit with five small globes, string along the bridge like Christmas lights. I'm laughing. Then it's as if there's an explosion and there's light everywhere, like I'm inside of it.

"Mark," Grace says right before the music of screeching tires and scraping metal. Which is followed by the sounds of our car flipping and rolling. The *crack* of bone breaking and glass shattering.

My head hits a window. I'm hanging upside down, the seat belt cutting into my chest. And Grace—Grace is next to me. Her eyes are open, and she's holding her breath. It is so quiet. I'm waiting, waiting to hear her breathe.

The image fades, and I keep moving forward on the bridge. I can't believe it's the last week of summer vacation. How did that happen? It's not like I'm dreading school, it's more like I've lost track of time. Or maybe time has lost track of me.

Cars occasionally drive by, but I'm mostly alone. I stop in the middle of the bridge, where a square concrete slab acts as a bench. I stand on it and reach up to touch the top of the black iron spikes of the suicide bars. I push down, but they're not sharp enough to pierce the skin. Even though I'm not super tall, 5'10", I easily scale the rail and climb over.

On the other side, I hold the bars and lean forward, like I'm a skier who has jumped and now flies through the air. The water rushes below. It's dark, but the light from the bridge and the surrounding buildings is enough to let me see the concrete below. If I hurl myself forward with enough velocity, maybe I can reach the trees in the arroyo.

It happened in the 1930s. Some distraught mom wrapped her baby girl in a blanket, kissed her, and threw her off the bridge before jumping after her. The mom died, but the girl was caught in the branches of a tree. She lived. I would have liked to have seen that. I picture the white blanket unraveling, trailing after her like white smoke, snagging in the tree.

I stretch my body out farther, though I hold tight to the rails.

"Grace!" I yell into the darkness.

No one answers back.

I try again. "Grace!" Not even an echo.

"It should have been me," I whisper.

I close my eyes and see her again, that blank stare. The guilt overwhelms me, and I wish I were the dead one. Really, it would be so easy.

I try to feel it, that space between wanting to live and wanting to die, as if it's tangible, someplace I can crawl into. I strain against the bridge and the air. Only my fingertips hold my weight.

The steel bar cuts into my fingers. My arms start to shake. I open my eyes.

Someday I will die, but not today. I climb over the bars and make my way back to the side road where I parked the car.

Three

shut off the engine and look up at my house. It's dark, except for the light in the kitchen, the one left on to scare away robbers.

Tap. Tap. Tap. I jump. Hanna's face peers at me through the car window. Her brown hair is pulled back into a high ponytail.

"What the hell?" I open the door.

"Nice seeing you, too, Mr. Grumpy Pants."

She nods, the sign for me to follow. I know I only have one choice, so I head after her. If I don't, I'll hear about it by not hearing about it, and Hanna's silent treatment is almost as bad as hearing about it.

I glance at my house. No movement. That's good. It means

the parentals are still asleep. In a couple of strides, I'm even with her.

"Couldn't sleep?" she whispers.

I shrug. She knows I go somewhere. She knows I come back. That's about it. And that's all she needs to know. I'm sure Hanna has her suspicions, but we don't discuss them.

"You?"

"Steve's over."

"Oh." Steve is her mom's boyfriend, some super-off-the-chart-brainiac designer who works at JPL, as in Jet Propulsion Laboratory. They do all kinds of high-tech things, like make spacecrafts and send them to Mars. He's decent, but it's got to be weird knowing your mom's having sex with the guy just a few doors down from your room.

"Want to stay at my house?" I ask.

She looks at me funny. "Yeah, I'm sure your parents would go for that."

"What? I'll sneak you out before they even wake up. They sleep in on Saturdays. Besides, it's not like you haven't stayed over before."

"True, but . . ."

"Right," I say. I know what she's thinking. Hanna used to have sleepovers with Grace, which made more sense. We are all—no, we were all—the same age: Grace and me sharing the same birthday because of the whole twin thing, and Hanna only a couple of months younger than us. We would all hang out until it was time for bed, and then I'd hear the two of them giggling through the wall between our bedrooms. Alone on the other side, I always wondered what they were laughing about, jealous that I wasn't in on the joke.

Hanna and I walk in the dark because there are no street-lights. The neighborhood is quiet. No one is peeking out at us through slightly parted curtains. Most people are asleep.

"Or we could just stay up all night," she says.

Up all night? I have nothing going on tomorrow—today, actually—except a couple hours of bass practice. I could technically lose a night and still make it up before school starts. It's not like I sleep much anyway. Chris gave me something to help, but it didn't. I needed a brain wipe, not a sleeping pill. So instead I walk the bridge, or I put on headphones and plug in my electric bass and play until it's morning. I probably wouldn't get any sleep tonight. Besides, Hanna and I are overdue for an all-nighter, so I agree.

Hanna opens the gate that leads to her backyard. She tries to be quiet, but the hinges let out a slow whine. She freezes and her green eyes look at me all huge as if we've just been busted.

We wait, but nothing happens. There's no Mom or Steve checking to see who's breaking in. We tiptoe over to a large wooden swing hanging from a huge oak toward the back of her yard.

I sit on the swing first, holding it still so Hanna can sit next to me. She's in her pj's: a pink shirt and sweatpants. She rolls the waist down to rest just below her hips. I'm supposed to act like I don't notice, but I do, every time. Just because we've grown up together doesn't mean I don't have a pulse. The white cord to her insulin pump, which she dubbed Pepe a couple of years ago, peeks out from underneath her shirt. She's always complaining about having to wear Pepe, how it ruins her style, but it's not like she has a choice. She was diagnosed with type 1 diabetes when she was six, and she has to keep a close eye on her sugar level.

Years ago, her mom walked Grace and me through what to do if Pepe started beeping and we needed to help her. I basically have to make her drink something high in sugar, like orange juice—that stuff is loaded. It can be funny when Hanna's low because she acts kind of loopy and stubborn, but it can get scary real fast. She had a seizure two years ago and an ambulance had to take her to the hospital. I teased her about faking being sick so she could get attention when she came home, but I was worried about her.

I glide the swing slowly back and forth with my feet. Hers don't even touch the ground, so she pulls her legs up to her chest and hugs them with her arms.

"What are you looking forward to the most?" she asks.

I smile. She knows *How are you*s are banned from conversation, but she's always finding a way to ask without saying the words. I should mind, but I don't. I kind of like that she checks in on me. "Tonight?"

"No, senior year, stupid."

"Graduating." Not that I have any huge plans. I'm supposed to apply to music schools this fall. But I don't know if that's what I want anymore. I don't know anything anymore.

Hanna punches me softly in the arm. "I'm being serious."

"So am I."

"I'm looking forward to all the lasts."

"The lasts?" I ask.

"Remember freshman year? When you started high school, there were all these firsts. This year, because it's all ending, there'll be all the lasts."

I'm quiet, so she continues like she has to explain it to me.

"You know, the last time you attend an opening year assembly, the last time you have to take math, the last time you go to a football game, the last time you ditch class to go shopping with your best friend . . ." Her voice wobbles and trails off. She doesn't say Grace's name, but I know that's who she means. I stiffen next to her.

To say Hanna and I are different is an understatement. Half

the time I don't even try to pretend to understand her. She cries so easily, like at movies or when she hears about someone getting bad news or when she's frustrated. Never sit in rush-hour traffic with her when she's late.

She cried when she found out about Grace. She had come to the hospital and collapsed into her mom when Jenny told them. I watched her and felt nothing. I kind of envied her for making it look so easy. Hanna cried a few times and then it was over. It was as if all the painful stuff on the inside came out and she was fine. I didn't know how she could do that, how she could just let it go. I didn't cry when Grace died, still haven't. I kind of went numb. At the funeral, I stood there amid all the tears, but I couldn't do it. Everyone took my dry eyes as quiet stoicism.

If I feel anything, most of the time it's anger. Chris tried to get me to cry in his office, but all I could think about was how his widow's peak came to such a sharp point in the middle of his forehead. It looked like a perfect arrow to direct my fist.

I hope Hanna doesn't start crying now. I don't think I can take it.

Changing the subject, I ask, "Remember the first time we stayed up all night on this bench?" Though as soon as I say it, I kind of wish I could take it back.

"Yeah."

"Eighth grade." The year I got into the school for the arts. The year Hanna and I almost kissed.

"Dad moved out."

I nod, waiting for it to hit.

"You tried to kiss me." She says softly. She's looking at her toes. Her nails are some dark color.

"I *gave* you a consolation hug. You were the one who turned your face as I bent down. In fact, I could say *you* tried to kiss *me*."

She laughs. "Oh man, that was embarrassing."

"Yes, I was embarrassed for you," I tease.

"Shut up," she says.

I push us faster on the swing, suddenly a little embarrassed for bringing it up.

I wasn't embarrassed that night. I was confused. It was late and Hanna sent me a text about her dad and asked if I could come over. Normally she would have texted Grace, but Grace was in Long Beach visiting our mom. I wasn't interested in spending two weeks with Mom and her new husband. Grace said I was being stubborn, for not wanting to go, but I didn't care. In my opinion, Mom made her choice years ago when she left. I didn't see the need to facilitate the façade, but Grace, well, she was the more forgiving one of us.

So I ran over to Hanna's and she was waiting for me in the backyard on the bench. She looked so small and scared sitting there. She was crying. I sat next to her and listened to her talk about her parents, about how she couldn't imagine life without her dad in the house.

My parents split up when Grace and I were seven. Mom left on a Friday after her nurse's shift at the hospital. I remember because we had plans to go camping that weekend, and Dad made Grace and me stay at Tita Christie's instead. We didn't understand what had happened. I still don't. All I know is that she left us.

Mom gave Dad full custody and eventually met this guy Will and moved about an hour away. Dad married Jenny a couple years after the divorce. The funny thing is that they both fell for someone white, not that I have anything against white people. They probably figured they'd tried marrying a Filipino first, and since that had been a mess, why not?

I could relate to Hanna's drama of screwed-up families. Most of the time our piecemeal family was cool. We did get Jenny out of the deal. When she first met us, Jenny brought me a CD of my favorite bass music and Grace some fancy colored pens. We liked her right away. At least I did. She knew about Edgar Meyer, an amazing bassist, and that gave her instant points. Later I found out that Dad had given Jenny the tip. Grace took a little longer to win over because I think she was still holding out for Mom to come home.

Sometimes it sucked. Mom and I still weren't on the best

of terms. But I always had Grace. I never had to go through it alone, not like Hanna. She was the only kid. She had all the pressure of dealing with the hurt and her parents on her own.

Hanna had a huge tear running down her face. I wanted to tell her that everything was going to be okay. No, I wanted to *make* everything okay for her. I reached out and wiped her cheek. I had never touched her that way.

"You'll be okay," I said, looking into her eyes, which were swollen around the lids, but still glossy and beautiful. She looked into mine and I wanted to kiss her. She wanted me to, because she moved a little closer and her eyes started to close. I knew what I was supposed to do. But this was different from playing truth or dare with Jessica. I'd only wanted one thing from Jessica last year. This was Hanna. The same Hanna I had been friends with since the fifth grade. The Hanna whom I knew as well as I did my sister. Hanna, who made me feel nervous and safe at the same time.

I panicked. I hesitated too long and broke the mood, so I pretended like I was just going to give her a hug.

We sat there all night, not talking, me with my arm around her, even after it started cramping. That's when I got confused. I started to think I loved, or at least really liked, Hanna, because there was no one else I would sit up with all night long, not even Grace.

• • • •

"I hope it's a good year," Hanna says. "I really need a good year."

"You'll have a great year," I say.

"Of course." She pauses and adds, "There's nothing to *fear*."

I rest the back of my head on the bench. "Depends on what's near."

"Or if it's all clear."

Hanna and I play the game that she, Grace, and I started years ago. Grace was usually the best. She had an ear for rhyme. She'd write these amazing poems, so it really wasn't fair to play with her. It was never stacked in our favor.

Tonight I win because it's only Hanna and me now, and I'm the last one awake. I don't mind that her head has fallen on my shoulder. She smells like Hanna, a little bit of sweat and ivory soap. I put my arm around her and rock us slowly back and forth on the swing. It's almost morning, but I don't want to wake her. I want to stay here as long as possible. I listen to her steady breathing and watch the orange glow of dawn creep over us and cover the sky like a blanket.

Four

The resonance of the electric bass hums against my body. It's taken an hour to get here, but now that I've worked out the notes on the page, I'm inside the music. This is where I feel the most clarity. I don't know many holy things, but I know this: Music is holy.

I've always had a thing for music. Dad calls it a gift. He started me on lessons when I was six and let me choose the instrument. I picked the bass because of its low and powerful sound. The bass sets the tempo and the feel. If a jazz band is a person, the bassist is the muscle. The drums are the skeleton. Guitars or keys are the limbs. Vocals add the facial gestures. At school, I alternate between upright and electric depending on the group I'm in.

I can't sing, though. Well, I can sing in a crowd, like "Happy Birthday" or to add a little backup, but I'm more comfortable behind an instrument. I have to take music theory at school, which does require some singing. Thankfully I'm not graded on the actual vocal quality, just that I know how to read the music.

I think I'm one of the few in class who actually enjoys the theory. It's like studying another language. Maybe I'm good at it because I know English and Tagalog. I'm not super-fluent in Tagalog, but I know more than just how to ask where the bathroom is. Any time I'm around the aunties, Dad's sisters, they make me practice with them. Tagalog is technically my first language, though I stopped speaking it outside the house in the first grade. It was hard enough when the other kids, mainly white because of the practically all-white suburb we used to live in, would see what Mom had packed Grace and me for lunch.

"*Longanisa*," I would say, as if they'd never seen sausage before. It's awesome, even though it makes your breath stink. And you burp it up all day. So I started asking Mom for peanut-butter-and-jelly sandwiches with the crust cut off, grapes, and a pack of chips.

After Dad married Jenny and we moved to Eagle Rock, which has a pretty good-size Filipino population, I still didn't speak Tagalog much. The aunties said I'd regret it when I got older, but I figured I'd regret lots of things by then, so add it to the list.

But music is the perfect language because everyone can speak it. It's not hindered by words. There's no room for misinterpretation. There's only the essence, the emotion of what we communicate to each other. Take sadness or anger or even joy. We try to explain how we feel, but there aren't always the right words, or the words we have fail. But with music, you can hear a piece and say, *Yeah, that's it. That's exactly how I feel.* Especially jazz. I love how it can make you feel really laid-back or even sad, but not feel despair.

Today the music I'm playing is all minor chords.

I sense someone in front of me and open my eyes. Jenny smiles at me.

"What?" I say loudly before remembering to take off my headphones. "Sorry, Jenny." I put the bass down next to its amp beside my bed.

"No problem. You hungry?"

"Yeah."

She hands me a fork and a plate of scrambled eggs, toast, and bacon.

"It's cold," I say, but eat it anyway.

"It's almost noon." Translation: *Get your butt downstairs earlier for breakfast.* "You up late?" she asks, watching me eat, leaning against my desk with her arms crossed in front of her. She's still got on her workout clothes—black leggings and a gray T-shirt—so it's probably been a slow morning. Jenny's in great shape, and works hard for it five mornings a week at the gym.

"Yeah," I say with my mouth full of bread.

"Mmm-hmm." She reaches out and touches my shirt. "Sleep in your clothes again? Didn't I buy you new pj's a week ago?"

She waits for me to answer, but I put some more food in my mouth. Jenny's not stupid. She cuts through the bull, but she's got a gentle touch. There's not much you can pull over her. I like that about her. You know exactly where you stand. This morning she's hovering between *I'm going to speak to your father* and *You can talk to me. I'm here for you.*

"Your dad left early. Someone called from the store."

Dad works as a district manager for a chain of department stores. He's always being called into work. It's cool because I get free clothes all the time. But it keeps him pretty busy, especially the past few months.

"He'd like us to have dinner together. You have plans?"

"I was going to hang with Sebastian later. Maybe get some practice in."

"I'm making chicken piccata."

"Okay, yeah, that sounds good." Jenny's best dishes are always

Italian, probably because that's her background. She's got tons of secret family recipes that she and her sisters fight over.

The first year Jenny lived with us, she tried to cook Filipino food, which Dad thought was cute. Grace reminded her each time that we didn't just eat Filipino food, which was true, but it was our comfort food.

Jenny started with *adobo*. Now, everyone knows that each family makes *adobo* differently, some with chicken, some with pork, some more dry. Jenny found a recipe that called for coconut milk. Mom never used coconut milk. I know she was trying to please us, but yeah, it didn't come out right.

I will say, Mom makes a perfect *adobo*, better than the aunties', though I'd never tell them that. Sometimes I'll order it at a restaurant. It's never the same. I explained it once to Jenny: *adobo*'s like Italians and their pasta sauce. She stopped trying after that. The aunties taught her how to make awesome *lumpia*, though, and she'll make that every now and then.

"Good. Dinner's at six p.m.," Jenny says.

We're discussing food, but we're not talking food. Jenny's subtext is, *We're worried about you. We want to spend time together, to act like we're a normal family. I'm making your favorite dish. Please try. For us.*

When Grace died, I thought I was going insane. I bailed on everything: school, friends, music. I started "acting out." After I screamed at Dad and Jenny to "Leave me the fuck alone" and slammed my fist into a wall, they set up appointments with Chris. Chris said I might be suffering from post-traumatic stress disorder, which I didn't believe. I know guys come back from war with that. I hadn't been in any war. Chris said PTSD could happen after any kind of trauma, and explained that it could make you emotionally detached, prone to bouts of anger and replaying the incident of trauma over and over.

I told Chris, "I lost my twin. She died. People die every day. It's called grief. People handle it."

"How do you think you're handling it?"

The way he said *handling it,* as if the words had quotations around them, set my mouth, and I didn't say anything for the rest of our time.

"Mom, zip me up!" Fern yells as she runs into my room. Fern is named after the girl in *Charlotte's Web,* one of Jenny's favorite books. She looks nothing like a little white farm girl, but the name somehow fits her. She takes after Jenny with her lighter olive skin tone, but she looks like Grace and me in the eyes and the dark hair. Jenny's more of a dark blond. When Fern smiles, the small space between her two front teeth is just like Dad's. She's the perfect Filipino-Italian-American girl.

"Is that how we ask?" Jenny says.

"Please?"

Jenny helps Fern with her blue princess dress.

Fern twirls in front of me. Today she's Cinderella.

Jenny fixes the bun in Fern's hair so that a couple of black strands are loose and frame her face. "Beautiful girl."

"You want to play princess with me, Mark?" she asks.

"Tempting," I say, "but I need to practice."

"You always say that."

"It's true."

She pouts. "Grace would play with me."

It takes everything inside of me to not throw my bass across the room.

"Fern," Jenny says, "why don't you go to your room? I'll come play with you in a minute." Fern's pink slippers scamper across the wood floor like little bunnies.

Jenny looks around as if she's working up the courage to say something. I speak up instead.

"She's just a kid." Kids talk and don't always know what they're saying. I remember this one time we were standing at a stop sign next to a very large man and Fern told me, "He's fat." I had been so embarrassed. The man could obviously hear her, but he didn't even look in our direction.

Of the two of us, Grace spent more time with Fern. I kind of treat her like she's an experiment, pushing buttons and pulling levers to see how she'll react. Fern is my sister, but our age gap is so huge, I feel more like an uncle than a brother. There is no way we could be as close as Grace and me.

Since Grace and I were twins, we shared more than blood and a last name. Most twins, I think, have this uncanny closeness. I've heard stories about the ones who can actually feel pain when the other is hurt. We didn't have any superpowers like that. We couldn't read each other's minds, though it wasn't for lack of trying. When we were kids, we'd sometimes practice for hours, staring at each other, flinging our thoughts across the room, but it never worked. But I did know *how* Grace thought. I knew how she felt. I knew how she'd answer questions, how she only liked nuts in ice cream and not in cookies.

And when Grace died, I knew rationally she wasn't here anymore. I knew she was gone. She *is* gone.

But I can still feel her. Sometimes she speaks to me. I'm not talking voices in my head, more like whispers of past conversations. It's like being an amputee with a missing arm, reaching out to scratch an itch or still feeling pain. Grace is my phantom limb. I told this to my friend Sebastian once and he understood it right away. It was the one true thing I offered to Chris in our sessions. He said to give it time, that eventually the feeling would go away. That pissed me off because what made him think I wanted it to go away?

Maybe it's because I've shared my life with Grace from

the very beginning, since we were pressed back to back in our mom's womb. The story is that when the doctor delivered us by C-section, we were holding hands. The doctor had to literally unclasp our fingers because I wouldn't or she wouldn't let go. I came out first, so Grace jokingly called me her big brother.

"School's almost here," Jenny says. "Looking forward to it or hating the idea?" I'm surprised to see tears in the corners of her eyes. Fern's comment about Grace must be the cause. I try not to show it, but the tears make me angry. I don't even know why, but I feel like breaking something again.

"More like neutral about it."

She holds out her hand for my empty plate. "Well, I loved senior year. Let me know if you need anything." I imagine dropping it and watching it shatter on the floor, but I give it to Jenny because I am *handling it* just fine.

After showering, I tell Jenny I'm going out and make my way over to Sebastian's family's Korean BBQ food truck. It's parked at one of their usual Sunday spots in Los Feliz.

Since it's lunchtime, there's a substantial line at the food truck. I go to the front, probably pissing off some people, but I don't care. I met Sebastian freshman year in jazz band. He's the drummer and I'm the bass player, so it's not really a surprise that we became friends. Now I'm practically family. Sebastian's dad sees me through the window and waves me away with a quick flip of his wrist, but Sebastian gives me a nod, the acknowledgment I was looking for.

I sit on a brick wall and wait for things to calm down. Their truck is very popular, and people follow it from place to place. Sebastian's family actually owns a couple in the area. They started with one in LA when the food truck craze hit years back and then expanded.

Sebastian eventually brings me a plate of beef ribs, rice, and kimchee and joins me on the wall. Sebastian's short, about 5'5". He's half-Korean and half-white, but all skinny.

"How's work?" I take a bite. Damn, it's good food.

"Crazy." He removes the black fishnet hat he has to wear. "What's going on?"

"Nothing."

"What does your dad put in this stuff?"

"Old family recipe," Sebastian says with a mock Korean accent, and smiles.

After Grace died, Sebastian came over with his drum kit and we played for hours until we were both sweating and exhausted. He didn't ask me any questions or tell me stupid stuff, like *She's in a better place* or *God needed another angel in Heaven.*

I hated that last one, because it didn't make any sense. Angels aren't former people, for one thing. Angels are their own separate beings. So there's no way that Grace is now an angel in Heaven. Maybe she is in a better place, but we don't really know that. We can't really say with certainty what happens after we die, where we go, if our souls live on or if they just evaporate.

Some people say that God has a plan for everything, and when life is going well that sounds good. But to think God's plan was to let a seventeen-year-old girl die in a car accident before she's really lived her life, before she was able to figure out why she's here in the first place, and leave me behind like a cruel joke—well, that would be one screwed-up plan by one screwed-up God. I believe in God—so did Grace—but not that kind of God. God isn't a sadist. God is supposed to be all loving and shit.

Grace's death was tragedy. Pure tragedy. No amount of explaining could erase the meaninglessness of her death. If I thought about it too much, I started acting like a person Grace would be disappointed in.

"I've been thinking," Sebastian says.

He's got that faraway look of his. The one that comes when he's going to get all profound about the universe. I prepare myself. "What?" I wipe my mouth with a small rough white napkin.

"With all this space and stars and galaxies, the probability of extraterrestrial life is a given. It's only a matter of time before there's contact. I hope I'm here to see it." He looks up as if he's expecting something to fall from the clear blue sky.

Sebastian's obsession with the stars and the idea of alien life apparently started in the sixth grade when an uncle bought him a telescope. He is a member of some club at the observatory. I tend to overlook his major geekiness because Sebastian is a kick-ass drummer and beat maker and my friend. I also indulge him in these conversations, because what else were we going to talk about?

"I've been thinking the same thing," I say with a bit of humor that isn't lost on Sebastian.

"I'm serious."

"No, really. I bet they're out there—aliens, I mean. They're, like, millions of miles away—"

"Light-years," Sebastian says. "Maybe even trillions."

"Lots of light-years away. And they're wondering if they are the only life-forms in the universe, except they only have to think it because they speak telepathically."

"It's plausible." Sebastian seems pleased with my response.

"You think they eat kimchee?" I ask.

"Maybe. You ready for school Monday?"

"Sure. You?"

"Yeah. Senior year. Should be cool, right?"

"Right." Though I feel more like I'm going through the

motions. If I were honest, I'd tell him I don't know how I'll make it through the first class.

"Come on. You can help me clean up."

I start to protest, but he points to my now-empty plate.

"Nothing's for free, man."

I follow Sebastian to the truck. No, nothing's for free. I toss my plate in the black trash bin. Most things come with a great cost.

Five

On Monday morning Sebastian and I sit in his car in the school parking lot. Normally I would have driven myself, but the car Grace and I shared was totaled in the accident. Sebastian agreed to be my ride to school until I got a new car. The insurance gave us plenty of money to replace the car, but I haven't gotten around to it yet. The accident was the other driver's fault. He had reached for something he'd dropped and swerved into our lane, hitting us head-on. He came out without a single scratch. I had to get stitches in my head and Grace was pronounced dead at the hospital at 8:43 p.m., but I knew that wasn't true. She died at the scene. I saw her. She never took a breath.

When the clock on Sebastian's dashboard turns to eight, he says, "Ready?"

"Yep."

Eleven minutes. I have eleven minutes to walk across the campus to my first-period class. Outside of the car, I pull my beanie low, sling my electric bass over my shoulder, and do a quick check in the passenger-side window. I changed my plugs from black to white this year. Something different. They're small. I don't want to have my lobes hanging down to my shoulders when I'm twenty-five or something, but I like the way they look.

I walk like I'm supposed to be here, with my shoulders back and head up. I look people in the eyes. I don't give them the option to avoid mine. The more normal I act, the more comfortable they'll be. In a few days, it'll be like nothing happened. I just have to get through today.

Stephanie comes up and puts her hand on my arm. "So good to see you, Mark." She gives a little squeeze. Even though Grace and I didn't go to the same school, everyone knows what happened last year on the bridge.

"You too," I say, and push past her, a smile on my face. Seven minutes.

I go to this high school for the arts, which is pretty cool and kick back, but demanding, especially during recital and concert times. I got in after auditioning in the eighth grade. It was the first time Grace and I were really separated. We had always attended the same school. Most of the time we were even in the same classes. She could have gotten in here for her writing, but she didn't want to apply. She preferred going to the same high school as Hanna.

The school day is divided. During the first half we function like a normal high school, with typical academic classes like English, math, and science. But the second half is different. The second half is playtime. We spend the rest of the day working in our artistic areas. It's a long day, some of us don't leave the campus till six, and sometimes it's tough managing everything, but we are there for a reason. We are doing what we love to do. We are artists first, brothers, friends, skaters, athletes, whatever, second. Freaks at any other school, I guess, except here, where everyone is a bit odd in their own way.

The school's not perfect. They still allow some assholes to attend, but overall it's cool.

Before first period, students stand in clusters, most of them according to disciplines. The theatre peeps hang near the auditorium. Musicians, my usual tribe, with their instruments in all shapes and sizes enclosed in black cases, lean against the doors of the music room. Fine artists have claim to the benches in the quad. Dancers get the spot underneath the huge tree at the top of the quad. Newbies wander and mix with the interdisciplinary students, who tend to move from group to group. Nothing has changed. Everyone's high-fiving and hugging and greeting one another as if a summer away has been hardly any time at all. For me, it seemed like an eternity.

"I'm that way." Sebastian points in the direction of his class. "You all right, man?"

"Yeah, see you in theory."

We part ways, and I head in the opposite direction.

"Santos!" Pete skates up behind me and smacks my head. "Glad to have you back!" he calls as he continues down the hallway.

I yell, "Punk!"

Pete's wearing a gray suit and pink bow tie. His long black hair is up in a bun on top of his head. His rollerblades make him, like, 6'4". Last year he experimented with a retro 1980s style; this year it looks like it'll be the '40s. He likes to think of life as performance art. The teachers don't seem to mind. Other than Sebastian, Pete was the only other friend I saw over the summer. A week after the accident, Pete and Sebastian sat on beanbags on the floor of my room with me, playing video games. The second time he brought some fried chicken and waffles and we watched a movie.

Two minutes. I walk down hallway and head for room 207.

"What's up?" I greet the guys waiting outside as if we just saw each other last week.

"Not much," Levon says. He's a talented dancer who can do it all: ballet, hip-hop, modern, and tap. Out of all the kids here, I expect to see him on TV some day.

"You have Mrs. Yenella for history?" I ask.

He nods. "I hear she's funny, but she makes you write research papers."

"See you inside," I say.

I open the door and enter the room. A short Latina woman is writing on the board. I head for an empty seat in the back corner before she can offer a greeting.

The bell rings.

I relax. I do the math. I only have 270 days. 6,480 hours. 388,800 minutes to go. I remember what Hanna said as I watch the clock. 388,799 minutes. *Here's to the lasts.*

Six

The brown box is beat-up and held together by a botched tape job. I can't tell if someone opened it and closed it back up or if it was tossed and abused on the journey to my house. The return address is the police station. Instead of opening it, I sit down next to it on the porch steps. Jenny's out somewhere with Fern and it's too early for Dad to be home, so I'm alone. It's just me and the box. I eye my skateboard leaning against the house and think about going to the park.

A door slams across the street and Hanna heads for our yard. I can tell she's pissed by the way she walks, with her head down and little, quick steps.

She plops next to me and pulls her cap low. Her sulking

effort is not lost on me, but it makes her look cute instead of seriously angry.

"Hey," I say.

"How was your first day?" she asks.

"I survived." People were a little weird, but I kind of expected that. Levon was right about the papers for my history class. There's one due in three weeks. My English teacher has decided to torture us right at the start with *Frankenstein*. I thought it'd be cool, but after flipping through the first pages I can tell it's going to be slow reading. I have a stack of new music for orchestra and jazz band. "You?"

"Okay. Are you locked out?"

"No."

"What're you doing?"

"Nothing."

She takes off her hat and lets her brown hair fall just past her shoulders, combing it with her fingers. I reach out and fix a section for her. Her hair is so soft. I let my hand linger a little, but drop it when she starts speaking again.

"Mom wants to talk with me later about Steve. But I already know what she's going to say."

"What?"

"She wants him to move in with us."

I wait for her to continue, not sure how to respond. I try to think of what Grace would say if she were here. Would she nod her head? Give Hanna a hug? That could get awkward or interesting. Maybe Grace would tell her what a bastard Steve is? No, she'd let Hanna talk.

Grace was a great listener. She wasn't an "uh-hum" or "yes" or "right" commenter throughout your story. She didn't wait until you took a breath, then immediately start speaking. She'd wait until you were completely done, look you in the eye, and say something profound, like *Tomorrow will be better than today*. So I wait for Hanna.

After a moment, she continues, "Steve's decent. I mean, he could be a complete asshole, but he's not. He always asks me about what I'm doing. Last week he brought me a bag of Skittles, not the regular kind, but the sour ones. You know, the ones I like. He remembered me talking about them. And he makes Mom happy. But moving in. That's serious. That changes things. He'll be living with us, as if we're a family. I don't know. Maybe I just need to get over myself, but . . ."

"But he's not your dad."

"When they first split, I used to imagine all these scenarios of them getting back together. Did you do that?"

I shrug. "I can't remember. Maybe. My mom left when I was a lot younger."

Grace was the one who would talk about Mom coming

back. She made up some story about how Mom was kidnapped and how we'd have to wear disguises and go and rescue her, like she was a princess in one of Grace's stories. She thought Mom must be scared. Why else wouldn't she have taken us with her? That had to be the explanation, because the other option was too painful. Over time Grace stopped talking about it.

"What's that?" Hanna asks, glancing at the box.

"A package."

"I can see it's a package. What is it?"

I shrug again.

She gets up and looks at the label. Behind me, I hear her open the door, and after a couple minutes she comes back outside with a pair of scissors. She sets the package between us.

After the accident, our car was taken as evidence and impounded. Supposedly the police collected our personal belongings from the car and mailed them to us after the settlement, but we never got them. Dad tried to follow up, and I remember him yelling into the phone after the package had gotten lost in the mail.

I don't make any effort, so Hanna cuts and rips through the packing tape. It takes some moments before she gets it open and when she does, she slowly removes each item and lays it out on the porch: one of my black T-shirts, Grace's purse, a small plastic bag with the car's registration and insurance, a pink flip-flop, my backpack from last year, some pens, a pack of gum, another small bag with change, Grace's phone. We stare at them. The last belongings associated with Grace.

I wonder where the other flip-flop is. *Was she wearing flip-flops that night?* I can't remember her feet. I suddenly need to get out of here. Hanna opens Grace's purse, and I want to grab my skateboard and bail, but Grace is my sister, not Hanna's. I can't let Hanna be the one rummaging through her stuff alone.

I pick up the phone and try turning it on, but the battery is dead. Dead like Grace. I place it back on the porch. The pack of gum is missing one piece. Opening a stick, I place it in my mouth. Cinnamon burns my tongue, but I keep chewing. *Was this her last taste before she died?*

Hanna pulls one of Grace's journals from the purse. Grace always preferred small notebooks that she could keep hidden away. I thought she should just use her phone. She said you couldn't write poetry and personal thoughts on phones. They required paper and pen.

Hanna looks at me, her eyes asking if she can read the journal. Part of me hesitates. Grace was always private about what she wrote, which is partly why I haven't gone through any of the journals in her room. Would this make Grace uncomfortable? Would she want us to know her real thoughts? It's dangerous reading someone's secrets. You could learn something that can never be unknown.

But if I read Grace's words—Grace's last entries—maybe they would replace the sound of the last word she spoke: my name. She didn't yell it. She said it as if I would know what to do, as if saying my name would make everything all right.

It didn't.

The oncoming car slammed into us, and then she was gone. She trusted me completely, and I failed her.

I nod for Hanna to go ahead, and she opens the journal and turns the pages slowly, with a kind of reverence, as if it's a book of scripture. I don't look at the words on the page. I can't bear to see Grace's handwriting, the way she combined printing with cursive. I watch Hanna's face, waiting for the tears, but they don't come. Instead, Hanna smiles.

"'Top Five Things to Do This Year,'" Hanna reads.

Grace was always making these Top Five lists, which she usually shared. Top Five Places to Eat. Top Five Places to Get Your Nails Done. Top Five Things Not to Do on a Friday Night. Top Five Guys to Avoid. Top Five Ways Not to Break Up with Someone. That last one had made me laugh. The number one reason was by text. I knew Grace got that from Hanna after Mike Salvatore dumped her in the ninth grade. His text message had read: **My mom said I'm too young for this relationship. LOL. Don't be**

mad. **See you around.** Hanna didn't tell me, but I heard it from Grace, who pretty much told me everything, especially when I pestered her about it. I thought it was hilarious, but I never said anything to Hanna, who moped around for two weeks after that.

Hanna reads the list. "'One: Train and run in a 5K. Two: Go bungee jumping. Three: Learn to surf. Four: Perform spoken word at a club. Five: Hike to the top of a mountain and watch the sunrise.'"

I'm not completely surprised by the list. I know Grace wanted to run. She started a couple of months before she passed. I thought it was because of River, though, this guy she was dating. He was a runner at her school, and I teased her about trying to impress him. But I can't see Grace standing in front of a mic reading her poetry. She was terrified to speak in front of people. She also hated the ocean. And bungee jump? She was scared of heights.

The list makes me wonder what else Grace kept from me, and I feel a twinge of betrayal that quickly morphs into sadness because she died before getting to do any of these things.

The night of the accident, Grace was pressing me for my own kind of wish list. I told her I don't think like that. I take life as it comes. She didn't believe me.

"You're way too driven, Mark," Grace said. "Come on, what's something you wish you could do, but you haven't yet?"

"I don't know."

"Tell me," she whined.

I let out a secret because it was Grace and Grace was good with secrets. She was also the one I wanted to tell first. Sharing things with Grace made them real. "I want to go to Berklee."

"In Boston?" Her tone was serious, as if she were thinking through the implications.

"Yep."

She was quiet, and I drummed along to the music on the steering wheel. She was processing. Boston was three thousand miles away. We'd never been that far apart before.

"Do it!" she said suddenly. The words came out in a rush. "You totally need to do it. I could go to Harvard, and we could be roommates."

"Harvard's in Boston?"

"Yes, Mark." She laughed at me like I should know these things.

"I don't think I should live with my sister in college. You'll scare away all the ladies."

She laughed even louder. "Yeah, right. Besides, what about Hanna?" She poked me in the ribs.

I stopped drumming and shifted uncomfortably in my seat. "What about her?"

"Oh please, she's, like, at the top of your wish list." She leaned her head against the passenger window and smiled.

"I don't have a wish list."

"Maybe not number one, but for sure, she's number two," Graces said right before I decided to take the route that led us to the bridge.

Usually I would have taken the freeway, but I knew how much she loved that bridge and how it was all lit up at night. I turned right.

The decision took less than a second. The neurons fired in my brain and my hands turned the wheel; that's how long it took. One small decision. But if I could take it back, I would.

"Mark?" Hanna asks.

I look at her in confusion because my thoughts are still with Grace. I stare at Grace's belongings on the porch and try to pull some meaning from them. On their own, they're insignificant: loose change, a matchless shoe, ID. When I try to string them together, they shout the glaring truth—that Grace is gone. I'm still here. And no matter how I try to arrange the fragments that Grace left behind, they'll never add up to anything whole again.

"I know it's crazy, but I think we should do it," Hanna says.

"Do what?"

"The list." She places her hand on the journal. "Grace's list."

I suck in my anger, wanting to control it because I know Hanna isn't trying to hurt me. "I don't know," I say, letting the air out slowly and counting to ten in my head.

"I know we were all supposed to say good-bye to Grace at the memorial when everyone said what they loved about her, but reading these words, *her* words . . . It's like she wanted us to find this." Hanna runs her hand over the journal. "I've wanted to do something for a while now, to honor Grace. And I want you to do it with me."

Even with me trying to be calm, my first impulse is to say no, throw everything back into the box, and trash it. Maybe I could put it back in the mail and it'd get stuck in some UPS loop. Part of me likes the idea of this package traveling—Singapore, New Zealand, Tibet, wherever, just as long as it keeps going.

But Hanna's eyes are intense, clear. I know the look. She doesn't need it, but she's asking for permission. My permission.

I stand up. I feel like this is a crucial moment, not necessarily life-changing, but important. I want to honor Grace, and as strange as it sounds, I know what Hanna means about getting the journal. Why now? Did Grace have something to do with it? Has she seen me walk the bridge late at night?

"So what do you want to do?" I ask. "Just go through the list?"

"Yeah. The one that'll take time to prep for is the race. I'll find a local 5K and enter us."

"You're going to run a 5K?" I'm doubtful. I've never seen Hanna run or work out, though she used to skate when we were kids and play soccer in middle school.

"We'd have to train, of course. Don't look at me like that. I can run if I have to. And you're going to do it with me."

I groan. "When? Like I have time."

"Early, then. Before school. Or on the weekends."

"We'll have to get started. It's already September."

"What do you mean?"

I point to the title of the list. *Top Five Things to Do This Year*. "We've got three months."

"Can I borrow this?" She holds up the journal.

"Sure."

Hanna beams at me and takes my hand. "Thank you, Mark."

"You're welcome." I squeeze her hand, but quickly begin to second-guess what I've just agreed to and let go. Holding her hand makes me feel things I don't deserve. Not now. Not like this. "We should put everything back. I don't want my parents to see all this stuff out."

Hanna folds the shirt and places it at the bottom of the box. I don't tell her it's mine. It's probably best to return everything just as it was. Before putting it away, I look inside Grace's purse. It's filled with her wallet, receipts, makeup, lip gloss, a stain-removing pen—that one makes me smile. She said that pen saved her clothes all the time because she was always spilling things on herself. Opening a side pocket,

I find a bracelet. It's silver with small hearts like dewdrops hanging from it.

"She loved that," Hanna says.

I stuff the bracelet inside the front pocket of my jeans, knowing what I should do, but not wanting to have a conversation with River. I've dealt with enough today. Hanna watches me, and I can tell she wants to say something.

"I don't want to talk about it," I say. "We just do the list, okay?"

"Okay, you don't have to talk. Only when you're ready." Her eyes are kind and deep and threaten to pull me under.

I almost respond with a biting remark, but I resist the urge to lash out at her.

We leave the box by the front door. I ask Hanna if she wants to go to the skate park, more out of politeness than out of actually wanting her to come. I kind of need to be alone. Thankfully she plans to start researching 5Ks.

"Oh, and I'm glad you survived your first day, Mark," she says before turning to go. "It can only get better, right?" She tosses the last word over her shoulder as she crosses the street.

"Right," I say back, and grab my board.

I skate for a couple of hours. No one bothers me. I see a few guys I know and we greet each other with nods and barely audible hellos, but I like it that way. No one talks to me, except through their boards. We have an understanding. Like them, I just want to skate.

I'm in my head with the familiar sound of the wheels thrashing concrete, trying to perfect moves I've been doing since junior high. I want to forget everything, everything except for this moment, me on my board in the park. But even here, where Grace's footsteps have never tread, I feel her absence, which makes her more present than ever.

Seven

t's only eight on a Friday night, and I'm already bored and lying in bed. Pathetic. I glance at *Frankenstein* on my table, but I have no desire to read. I hear Hanna playing her violin from across the street. I haven't heard her practicing in a while. She's efficient, but she'll never play in an orchestra. She doesn't have the discipline, not that it fazes her. She likes playing when she wants, and it doesn't matter if she only plays for herself. She told me once that if she had to practice every day for hours like I do, it would kill the fun for her.

I told her it would kill me not to.

My phone rings. I check the number and let it go straight to voice mail. Mom's persistent. I'm not sure what she expects from me. Like we're supposed to have phone conversations and send each other text messages with smiley faces because I'm her only kid left. Not going to happen.

The last time Mom and I spoke was at Grace's funeral. She clung to me, her eyes red and swollen from crying. She acted as if she cared so much, as if she and Grace were so close, and I just couldn't take it. I told her to leave me alone. Mom was hurt, but I didn't care. She rejected me first, years ago.

She leaves a message, but I press delete.

I log into my account at Twinless Twins, a group for people like me who have lost a twin. Carol, the nurse at school, told me about them last year when I was sitting in her office, refusing to be in class. She was having trouble with a crossword puzzle and I gave her the answer: Brandenburg Concertos. She had smiled, given me a lemon lollipop from the jar she kept on her desk, and told me about the website. After lurking around the site, I became a member about two months ago and have met some people. We message one another every now and then.

One's this older lady, Sandy, who lives in Detroit. She lost her twin when she was a kid. She told me how, for a long time, she could only fall asleep with one of her dead sister's shirts by her pillow. She still has these moments when she's in the house and has this feeling as if she's lost something, like her keys or jacket or glasses.

I picture her, short gray hair, chunky in a blue tracksuit, getting on her hands and knees, looking underneath her couch, opening her drawers. Finally she stands in the middle of the room and realizes she's looking for Stephanie, her twin. Sandy says she used to cry, but now she smiles and says things like, "Oh, you got me that time, Steph. Always playing tricks on me."

Even though I think Sandy's a little crazy, I get it. I have that feeling all the time, like I'm this walking jigsaw with a missing piece. Sandy told me that I have to remake the puzzle.

Don from Providence, Rhode Island, is a little closer to my age. He's twenty-six. He told me he had to learn to breathe again after his twin, Seth, died. Don would get these terrible chest pains, especially at night, as if he'd forgotten how to breathe. He started counting: breathe in, one, two; breathe out, one, two. This helped him get the rhythm right.

Tonight I have a couple of messages in my box.

Mark,
I had this dream. In it I saw Seth again. We were at the cabin my family had when we were kids. We were outside playing, throwing around the football. I told him to go long and he took off running, not even looking over his shoulder. In the last second, he turned and the ball slid into his hands. It was beautiful. Seth jumped up and down and kept

saying, "Did you see that, Don? Did you see me? Who's number one?" He smiled so big as he ran toward me. I woke up. It was a good dream.

Don

I haven't told anyone about the group. I'm not sure what they'd think. I like that it's my own thing. Maybe it's weird to be talking to total strangers, but at the same time it makes perfect sense. They get me in a way that my parents, Hanna, even Sebastian can't.

Mark,

To answer your question with another question, are we ever really whole? We're all broken in some way. Tell anyone who wants you to get over it to go to hell, sorry for my language. Kristen died five years ago, and I wanted to kill everyone who told me I just needed time. You know what time does? It makes me older when Kristen isn't. You know what's the most tragic thing? Getting older than your twin. But you're not alone. There are people here who get you.

Are you coming to the LA meet-up next month? If so, I'll see you there.

Greg

Twinless Twins hosts these meet-ups once a month in my area, and then a big conference in the summer where they talk about dealing with loss and grief and anger. I'm thinking about going. It's also for family and friends. Maybe Hanna or Sebastian would come with me.

I write Greg back and tell him maybe.

I get into bed and try to go to sleep. One, two, breathe in. One, two, breathe out. After what feels like a couple of seconds, I hit the vibrating alarm next to my head—12:01 a.m. I listen for noise in the house, but there's nothing. I grab my shoes from the floor next to the bed, knowing now to wait to put them on after I'm out the front door. I made the mistake of wearing them down the stairs one night, and Jenny pushed open her door and peeked out into the hallway. I froze halfway down the stairs, hoping that the darkness covered me. I waited until she slowly closed her door, then kept going.

Outside, the air is warm with a hint of the approaching fall. Apple-picking time. Every year we go to the mountains to a farm where we each get a white paper bag with a little handle and pick as many apples as we can fit into the bag. It's kind of cheesy, but Grace loves it. She *loved* it.

We always stop at the same restaurant on the way home. We drive to it with the windows down because you can smell the baked apple pie from, like, a mile away. Grace, Jenny, Dad, me, even Fern, each get our own slice with a huge scoop of vanilla ice cream. It's hard to find moments when everyone's happy, but this is ours, our snapshot as some magazine family.

This year none of us has mentioned going. It wouldn't really be the same. We should probably cancel Thanksgiving and Christmas too. I can't imagine trying to sit through turkey and green-bean casserole without Grace.

I'm sitting on the front steps, lacing my shoes, when a car pulls up in front of Hanna's house. The passenger door opens, and I hear Hanna's laugh. She gets out and stands on the sidewalk, waving as the car drives off. She watches the car until it turns at the end of our street. Then she looks at my house, and I lower my head, hoping that she won't see me, but no such luck.

"Spying on me now?" she says quietly as she approaches.

She's wearing one of her best outfits: black skinny jeans and a tight striped shirt. It's the same outfit she wore to the concert we went to over the summer when she was on one of her *Let's go and do something fun to try and act normal* missions.

"You wish," I say, and stand. I meet Hanna by my dad's car. "Who was that?" I nod toward the end of our street.

She hesitates. "River."

As soon as she says his name, I'm angry and something like shame rises in the back of my throat. Because now I've got this picture of the last time I saw him. He was lying on the ground, not even fighting me back as I pummeled him. He looked at me with pity, and that's worse than anything.

"I don't want any shit tonight, okay?" The words are out before I can think through what I'm saying.

She tenses and puts a hand on her hip. "You don't get to do that."

"Whatever," I say, and brush past her to open the car door.

She blocks me. "You act like I've done something wrong."

"Move," I say.

"Make me."

She glares at me, and I can see she's going to start crying.

I want to tell her I'm sorry. I don't want to be this person. I want to say that I don't know why I'm being cruel, but her tears just piss me off even more. Why does she always have to cry?

"Hanna, please move. I don't want to hurt you."

"Too late," she says. She walks away. I touch the handle, but I don't open it yet. I know that if I drive away, something between us will break. And I don't have many relationships that aren't broken. I hate to admit it because I don't even know what it means, but my relationship with Hanna is one thing that I can't have broken.

"Wait."

Hanna stops in the middle of the road.

"Come with me," I say.

"What?" She turns but not before I see her wipe a tear from her eye.

"You want to know where I go, right?"

She nods.

"I'll show you."

She folds her arms across her chest. "Say it first."

"I'm sorry." I don't really feel sorry, but Grace said that sometimes saying it is a good first step. Sometimes you say the words because it's the right thing to do for the other person. And standing here in the middle of our dark street, Hanna needs to hear the words.

I move toward her and touch the side of her arm. "I'm sorry," I say again. I search her eyes until she drops her gaze.

"Okay," she says. "Where are we going?"

I put my finger on my lips and lead her to the car.

Eight

park in the usual spot, along a quiet street near the base of the bridge.

I turn off the engine, and say, "Surprise."

"I thought..." Hanna's voice wavers like she's on the verge of crying again.

"What?" I don't let her finish. "Disappointed I'm not hiding out at some strip club?" My tone is harsher than I intend, but I can't stand the crying.

"Sort of," she says, and sniffles. "Or that you were part of some secret spy ring."

I laugh. "Let's go."

I lead her to the top of a narrow path that takes us to the bridge. It's easy to miss. I drove by it the first couple of times I came.

The trail is only wide enough for one person, so I go first. It switchbacks through bushes and thick trees.

"I've never been down here," Hanna says.

I shine the light from my phone at Hanna's feet. "Watch your step. There's a big rock." I reach out and take her hand to help her down.

"Thank you."

She lets go as soon as she gets her footing. I kind of wish there were more rocks. I'm not used to having anyone with me, so I feel the pressure of being a tour guide.

"Lots of people run or walk here. The path connects to the Rose Bowl. Of course, most people come during the day." At the bottom of the hill, the pathway opens, exposing us to skinny trees whose pale bones cast eerie shadows. At night it's creepy, a perfect spot to set a horror movie or Stephen King novel. I almost expect a zombie to jump out at us.

Our feet crunch on decaying leaves as we walk, making it impossible to hide our presence from anyone within a mile of hearing. I notice Hanna walks very close to me, as if she's a little scared, though she wouldn't tell me that. Hanna is strong for a girl. She doesn't let much bother her, except maybe her mom. They've had some killer fights. I can hear them sometimes through my open window. The next day Hanna acts like everything's fine, even though it isn't. She used to come talk to Grace about it.

I'm beginning to regret bringing Hanna here. I don't want to have to explain myself.

"Wow," she says. "It's so big."

She's referring to the base of the bridge. She's right. The bridge's chunky legs are curved like the base of a very old grandfather clock. The design looks like it could be in 1920s Paris or something. The globed street standards, which line both sides of the bridge in clusters of five every thirty yards or so, look like small floating full moons from where we are.

There's an old walkway lined by a stone wall that we take. We climb the crumbling rock steps and make our way to the concrete slab of the bridge's foundation and dam for the Arroyo Seco riverbed. Behind us, there's a spot where the water pools before it moves down into the channel. Most of the time there's hardly any water here, except for during rainy seasons, when flash floods can come through. Tonight the water trickles from the pool.

I sit down on the ledge. The concrete is cold through my jeans. Hanna sits next to me. "So, what do you do here?"

"It's just a good place to think. Listen." The cars speed by in a kind of syncopated rhythm above us. The water moves below. Sometimes the leaves on the bushes rustle. "People say there's ghosts here."

"Have you ever seen anything?"

"No, but I read about how ghost hunters have come here to try to catch them on film. It's stupid." Ghosts are just pieces of memory. They haunt us because we don't want to forget. We are the ghost makers. We take fragments of the dead and project them onto shadows and sounds, trying to make sense of loss by assigning it a new shape. Ghosts aren't real. Dead is dead. There is no getting someone back.

I'm starting to forget the small things. The way Grace smiled at me. How her voice sounded when she was angry. What color nail polish she wore. Her smell. Smell is supposed to be our sense with the strongest ties to memory. Sometimes I pull out one of her shirts to remind me of her scent because I can feel Grace slipping from me. And I'm terrified of what that means.

"He just wanted to talk," Hanna says.

"Who?"

"River. It's hard on him, too."

I can't remember Grace's laugh correctly either. Did she let it out all at once or did it build? I picture her playing tag with Fern. Suddenly I can hear it again. Her laugh came in quick spurts, like a motor being revved before it gets going.

"You should talk to him," Hanna says.

"Maybe," I say, though I have no intention of speaking with River again. Our last encounter, even if it was my fault, hadn't gone well. With Grace dead, I figured I'd never see him again. I didn't count on Hanna bringing him back into the equation. I didn't count on finding the bracelet. I get up. "Let's keep moving."

We make our way back to the arroyo and walk along the pathway, following it to the top of the bridge.

The air up here is cooler with a thin layer of fog. As far as I can tell, we're the only ones on the bridge. Hanna has her arms wrapped around her middle, so I take off my jacket and put it over her shoulders. She starts to protest.

"Stop it. You're cold. No arguments." I rub her arms.

"But now you'll be cold."

"I'm fine."

She leans in and rests her head against my chest and I wrap my arms around her. My heart races, and I try to remain very still. The last time Hanna and I hugged was after Grace's funeral. She was the one who reached for me, and I just stood there.

She starts to shake. And I can't tell if it's because she's upset or cold.

"You okay?" I ask with my mouth close to her ear.

"All good," she says, and pushes away. We start walking again.

"This is amazing at night. This bridge makes me feel like we could be in London." She lowers her voice. "As if Jack the Ripper is going to walk toward us." She grabs my arm. Hanna's like that. She's always pretending, making up scenarios. Most people stop that when they grow up, but not Hanna. She'd probably be a good writer one day—well, if she actually liked to write. Writing, of course, makes me think of Grace. Everything leads to Grace.

"It's safe," I say, and I link my arm through hers.

"You'll protect me?"

"With all my secret ninja moves," I say.

"I knew it! You *are* a spy. Explains a lot."

We both laugh.

"Yeah, the first Filipino assassin."

A car drives by.

"What time is it?" she asks.

I look at my phone. "One thirty."

"I should get home. Mom will freak if she wakes up and doesn't find me in my room. Plus it's way past curfew. We could get in serious trouble."

"She checks on you at night?" I wonder if Jenny or Dad check on me. If they do, they don't say anything.

"Sometimes. I hear the door open, but I pretend I'm asleep. Are you still seeing Chris?" she asks, casually, of course, but I know it's her way of trying to get a read on me.

"No. Last session was two weeks ago."

"So you're finally free."

"Unless you go telling someone about tonight."

She pushes her shoulder into me. "You know I wouldn't do that. And thank you."

"For what?"

"For showing me where you go. You didn't have to."

"Yep." I open my arms wide and spin around as if I'm taking in the whole street. "Big secret revealed. Mark Santos is a midnight bridge stalker."

"At least you don't go around dressing up in a mask and tights like a vigilante."

I look at her, surprised. "You really think I'm that crazy?"

"We're all that crazy," she says dryly, and does a little dance as if to show her crazy side.

"Nice moves," I say.

"I was thinking of something Grace used to say yesterday," she says.

My body tenses as if she's going to hit me with her words.

"Remember how she'd say, 'Whatever happens, happens'?"

"Did she?" I ask. I think about climbing the bars. If Hanna weren't with me, I'd be over them right now. But she'd probably freak out.

"All the time, you know that! And I found myself saying it to someone at school yesterday. This girl was telling me about how she wants to get into this college and she's all nervous about it, and it just came out. But it wasn't like I was saying it. I heard Grace's voice in my head. And then I kind of laughed because it's as if a part of her is still here."

I'm listening, but not listening, hoping she'll be done talking soon. I thought it'd be okay bringing Hanna here, that I was ready, but I'm not. I just want to get out of here. I sense Hanna is getting upset as she fidgets next to me.

"Why do you do that?" she asks.

"What?"

"Go somewhere else when I bring up Grace."

"I'm right here next to you. I haven't gone anywhere."

"I mean, in your head. It's like you won't ever talk about her, like you don't want me to bring her up around you."

"What the hell am I supposed to say?"

"I don't know. Something. Anything. It's like you want us all to forget her."

My head hurts. I want to tell Hanna to shut up, especially because I can tell she's going to get emotional. Why can't she see that I just want to be left alone? Why does this have to be about her?

"I miss her," Hanna says. "Do you know how hard it is to be back at school without her? I keep thinking I'm going to run into her by her locker, or see her round a corner. That she'll walk into class. I miss her every day. We had so many plans for senior year.

And now that's all I have, just these stupid plans that we'll never get to do together."

I stare at the cracks in the blacktop, at the gum stains and dirt. I imagine dried blood, my sister's blood, smeared across the pavement. But this isn't the spot. I know the place. It's a few paces up ahead.

"I can't," I say.

"What?"

"I can't talk about it, about her."

"Well, I need to," Hanna says. "And there's her list. I don't want to feel like that's a bad thing. I want to remember her. Grace was my best friend. I loved Grace."

I bend over and hold my head in my hands, trying to steady it and my stomach. The bile rises as if I'm going to throw up. Hanna rests her hand on my back, and I want to shrug it off, but I don't, because even though I'm mad, her touch feels good. It shouldn't, though; nothing should ever feel good again. I hear her sniffle, and I can't take her tears. I want to scream.

I stand up. "Let's go."

"Mark?"

"What, Hanna? What do you want me to say? Grace is fucking dead. Dead. Okay? You want me to say that I come here to try and what? To find her? Maybe her spirit is still here? I don't know. The truth is, I'm here and she's gone. Do I want to jump? Do I want to end it now? I don't know. I'm alive, and that's great. That's fucking great. But she's dead. Grace is dead, and I know that makes you sad, and that makes you want to cry, but you can't even imagine how I feel. I don't want to talk about it, not with you, not with my family, not with Chris, not with anyone. So back off."

Her eyes, which widened when I started yelling, now narrow like the tip of an arrow. "Grace may not have been my twin sister, but she was like a sister to me."

We glare at each other until Hanna raises her finger and points it at me. "You don't own the market on grief, Mark. So you're the one who needs to back off."

She drops her hand and starts walking away from me. I follow her back to the car, and we drive home in an angry and sad silence.

Nine

peek out of my blinds at Hanna's room across the street. Hers are closed. After sleeping off my anger, I'm now laced with guilt, which is why I have my phone in my hand to text her. Hanna shouldn't have pressed me like that. She knows better. But I know better too. I don't think I've ever used that many F-bombs with Hanna. Grace always made fun of me when I cussed, telling me it was proof that she was smarter. She said it didn't take any creativity or intelligence to swear, until she went through a phase sophomore year when she hung out with some UK exchange students. Grace walked around saying, "Bloody hell," all the time, and the ban on swearing was tentatively lifted as long as I used an accent.

I need to apologize to Hanna, but don't know how. I send out an exploratory message.

Hey

I wait a few minutes. Nothing. I think about sending another text, but I smell bacon. It's enough to get me to throw on some clothes and go downstairs. Everyone's sitting at the table in the kitchen nook. I don't look at the empty chair in the corner, but I know it's there.

"Mark, have some breakfast. Jenny's made ricotta pancakes," Dad says. Late Saturday-morning breakfasts are one of our family rituals. Even when Dad gets called in to work, Jenny loves making a big breakfast. She's always trying out new recipes on us.

"Fancy."

"Ricotta makes everything better," Jenny says. She gets up to serve me a plate.

"I can get it, Jenny," I say, and she sits back down. "There isn't garlic in here, is there?" I ask.

Jenny sticks her tongue out at me. "Funny guy."

I am only sort of kidding. Jenny uses garlic like most of us use salt. During dinner, no matter what's cooking, the air is infused with either sautéed, baked, or fried garlic.

"Mark, see what I drew?" Fern says. She holds up a picture next to her half-eaten plate of food.

"Cool," I say.

"It's our house." She picks up a blue crayon and begins drawing stick figures.

I sit next to her and take a bite of my pancakes. "These are great. Thanks, Jenny."

Jenny smiles a little too widely and looks at Dad, making me stiffen. I know they are concerned about me, but I'm tired of feeling like a lab rat, like everything I do is being watched, measured, and analyzed. This morning I'm doing well. I can tell by the glances she and my dad keep giving one another. I can hear their thoughts: *He's eating. He's saying please and thank you. Maybe he's back to normal.* As if there will ever be a normal again.

"What're your plans today, Mark?" Dad asks.

I shrug and check my phone. Still no text.

"We're heading over to the park," Jenny says. "You want to come?"

"Yay!" Fern says. "Can we go to the big one with the swings?"

"Yes," Jenny says.

"Actually I'm meeting the guys later to practice," I say, which isn't really true. But I was planning on calling Charlie, a guitarist I met at the skate park, and Sebastian to see if they had some time, for our band, The Distorted. Although I don't really know why I bother. We've been together for more than a year and we haven't played a single gig. Well, unless you count Sebastian's cousin's eleventh birthday party. Sebastian told us he booked a paying gig, and I think all Charlie and I heard was "paying," so we didn't ask for the details. When I pulled up to a backyard decorated with pink and white balloons and streamers, I considered bailing, but Sebastian met me at the curb with the birthday girl, who was all smiles. She wore a white dress and looked at me as if I were a rock star, so I got out of the car and asked where to set up.

We got paid $150, which we split three ways. They fed us too. By the end, we had twenty-six eleven-year-old girls worshiping us. Not bad for an afternoon. If you get them when they're young, you'll have them as a fan for life.

"Want to help me, Mark?" Fern says.

I don't really, but I pick up a yellow crayon and add a big sun to Fern's drawing. She has five stick figures standing in front of the house.

"Okay. In that case, can you make sure you clean the bathroom and your room today?" Dad asks.

"Yep." I can do this: be the good son, be a good brother. I glance at Fern. I've got another sister left.

"And your mom called again," Dad adds. "She says she's been trying to reach you. She wondered if you changed your number."

"I might have gotten a text or something. No message, though," I lie.

Fern writes DAD and MOM underneath the figures in the middle.

"It would be good to call her soon," he says.

"Yeah, okay." I have no intention of calling Mom, but I say what he wants to hear.

Jenny begins to clear the table. My dad gets up to help her. He places his hand on her shoulder and squeezes, probably because we're talking about Mom. Jenny smiles at him.

Fern writes my name underneath a figure, and I write Grace's name underneath the last one. Fern has drawn her with a triangle, like she's wearing a skirt, even though Grace never wore skirts. Her hair is black and shorter than it should be. I give it some length. I also add some lashes to her eyes and make her smile a little more even.

Fern catches her breath. "That looks just like Grace. You are a good drawer. Look, Mom!"

Jenny comes over to the table. "Yes, it does. Just like Grace." She places her hand on the figure, and I have to look away. "Let's get you ready for the day."

They leave and my dad stays at the sink with the water running, even though he's finished rinsing the dishes. His shoulders are hunched over. I'm trying to think of something to say, but my phone buzzes.

Hey

I'm sorry, I type, and get up from the table. This time I mean the words. "Bye, Dad," I tell him, and head back upstairs, leaving him at the sink. He doesn't respond.

You should be.

I know.

Me too

Come over

When?

An hour?

Maybe

An hour and a half later the doorbell rings. It's Hanna, standing there with her hands in her jean pockets.

"Well?" she asks when I open the door.

I smile, hoping that will be enough to win her over, but she kind of pouts. I can tell she's going to make me work for it.

"I said I was sorry."

"True," she says, and walks past me into the house. She takes off her shoes and throws them into the shoe basket by the front door before making herself at home on the couch in the living room. "Where is everyone?"

"Park." I think about joining her, but I sit across from her on the love seat.

"You didn't want to go?" She asks me all formal, like I'm being interviewed for some after-school job.

"Would you?"

"Probably not."

Our conversation is stilted as if there's something still

unfinished between us. I consider apologizing again when she stands up.

"You have anything to eat?" She heads for the kitchen.

"Yeah. You feeling okay?"

"Just a little low." And right on cue, her pump beeps. "All right, Pepe," she says, and pats her side. "Mama's coming."

Whenever her sugar levels are too low or too high, Pepe makes a soft beep. Hanna says he's just temperamental. Sometimes she sets Pepe on silent so she doesn't have to explain to people why she's beeping.

I pour her a glass of orange juice.

"Thanks," she says. "Maybe my sugar's fine. I could just be PMSing."

"Aww, man, why'd you have to do that?"

"What?" She hops up and sits on top of the counter, as she's been doing since we were kids. She swings her legs back and forth and drinks the juice.

"If I were to say that, I'd never hear the end of it."

"It's not like I asked you to get me a tampon or anything."

I put my hands over my ears. "Not listening." She knows this kind of talk freaks me out. Some things a guy just doesn't need to know. Grace used to try to discuss her womanly problems with me too. I guess she and Hanna thought it was funny to see my reaction.

Hanna pulls a book from her back pocket and tosses it to me. It's Grace's journal.

"Listen, Mark," she begins. "If you don't want to do the list, I understand." She avoids my eyes. "She probably just wrote it not thinking that she'd actually do these things. It's not like she thought anyone would read it and follow through. I don't want to push you. So . . ."

Hanna puts the empty glass down and jumps off the counter. She reaches out and touches my arm as she passes me, and the walls within me start to crack.

"No," I say.

"No?" She turns around.

"I mean, let's do it."

Hanna studies me, and I give her my best *I'm serious* look.

"Okay," she says, and smiles. "Let's start training for the run. Mornings? Six a.m.?"

"That early?"

"I need time to get ready for school. You said—"

"Okay. Okay. Six a.m.," I say, wanting to avoid another confrontation.

"One other thing. If you do read that"—she points to the journal—"you can't take it personally. Grace would never say half of those things aloud in real life. She never meant for us to read it, that's for sure."

"Why? What's in there?" Hanna's caution makes me nervous.

"Just stuff. Nothing damaging, more unfiltered. Thanks for the juice."

She heads for the front door and I don't even bother to see her out. Even if I wanted to, I don't think I can move.

The journal is small and so light, but now it feels heavy in my hands. Hanna's got me curious, even though I think she meant to deter me from reading it. That's the thing, though: Once you know you shouldn't do something, you kind of want to do it even more. I flip through and skim a poem. When I turn the page, the first line catches my attention.

I hate that I'm always being compared to Mark.

Okay, Grace, don't sugarcoat it or anything. Love you too. But I keep reading.

He's so good in music; why aren't you, Grace? I can't help that I'm not a genius musician. I remember when we were little, Mom and Dad used to dress us in color-coordinated outfits. Both of us had those ridiculous straight bangs. Mark got that bowl cut. Ha ha. Score! At least Mom let me have long hair.

We were always "the twins." The twins this and the twins that. One entity. Don't get me wrong, I love Mark. He's funny and talented and easy to talk to. He's there for me when I need him and vice versa. But sometimes I wonder what it would be like to be totally on my own. Sure, I've been lonely before, but with Mark, I know I'll never be alone, not really. It's a twin thing.

I wish I could be free, kind of like when we switched high schools. Thank God for that, at least I get some break. I like having my own friends. My own life.

That's how it'll be in college. I'll go away, and so will Mark. We'll start over. We'll text and call, but we'll reinvent ourselves. We'll still be twins, but no one will know me as part of Mark and Grace. I'll just be Grace. I can't wait.

I slam the journal shut. She got her wish, except I'm the one without a twin. I'm just Mark. I suddenly hate Grace. I take Hanna's empty juice glass and throw it. The glass breaks against the wall. I leave the shards on the floor, not caring what Dad and Jenny will say.

Ten

quickly pull a T-shirt over my head as Sebastian honks again
out front. I don't have time to brush my hair, so I grab my
usual brown beanie.

"Mark! Sebastian's outside!" Jenny yells from downstairs.

"Coming!"

After Hanna and I went for our first run, when we ran
maybe a mile—well, more like ran/walked a mile—I thought
that Hanna would change her mind about the 5K. I was wrong.
We've been at it for over a week, and I'm actually sore. I've got
a lot more respect for runners. I know my body will adjust, like
building calluses on my fingers from playing the bass and guitar.
I don't even notice them anymore, but at first they hurt to the
touch. I try not to wince as I step down the stairs.

At the bottom, Jenny holds out a brown paper bag with my lunch in one hand and a paper towel with a bagel and cream cheese in the other. I know I should tell her that she doesn't need to make my lunch anymore, that I can do it, but I like that she still wants to take care of me.

"Mark! Hugs!" Fern says, and jumps at me. I bend down and pat her on the back. Since Grace died, she kind of freaks out at good-byes. Any time you leave the house, she'll give you at least three hugs before you get out the door.

Sebastian honks again.

"Will you tell Sebastian not to disturb the neighbors anymore?" Jenny says. "He can get his butt out of the car and ring the doorbell."

Today I need my upright, so it takes a little maneuvering to hold my bagel, my bag, and my bass, which I carry like a backpack.

"I will. Sorry, Jenny."

"Have a great day."

"Hugs!"

I can't bend down, so Fern wraps herself around my legs. And this is how I shuffle to the door: with Fern attached to me like a small squid.

"Dude. We're going to be late!" Sebastian snaps as I put my bass in his backseat.

"Relax. We'll be right on time."

Sebastian hates being late, and he hates when I tell him to relax. He acts like he's the most chill person, but he's got all of these rules, and you don't find out about them until you start to break them. Like the late thing. I didn't fully grasp his obsession with being on time until he became my ride to school.

"And can you lay off the honking? You're starting to piss off Jenny."

Sebastian turns up the music as an answer. It's one of his beat tracks. Not only is Sebastian one of the most talented drummers I've played with, but he's also sick at composing. He does all the instruments on his computer.

"Seriously, get up earlier or something."

"I'm up at six. Hanna and I are training for a 5K."

"Wow, I knew you had it bad, but—"

I cut him off. "It's this thing she wanted to do for Grace."

Sebastian turns down the music. I tell him about the package from the police department with Grace's journal and her Top Five.

"I'm in. We can go bungee jumping at this place my cousin went. It's not too far. You hike a couple of miles to some bridge over a river. I'm off in a couple of Saturdays if you want to go."

I look out the window at people sitting in their cars on the freeway, just like us. They're listening to music, talking. This is good. I can do this: ride with Sebastian to school, talk about Grace, be normal.

"You'll have to speak to Hanna. She's got some plan."

"I'm not going in the ocean after October. We should get Charlie to take us. I don't have a wet suit. Do you have one?"

"Yeah. Can you turn the music back up? I love this track. When'd you do it?"

"Last night."

He turns it up, and I'm lost in the beats. I'm glad for the distraction. I hadn't planned on telling Sebastian about Grace's list. Now he's talking about bringing Charlie. It's becoming a production. I just wanted to do the five things and not make a big deal about it. I close my eyes and focus on the music, letting it take me to another place where I'm creating bass lines and a melody, a place where I'm safe.

During lunch, Sebastian asks if I want to go with Pete and him to get some cheap tacos at the truck up the road. We have an open campus, so most of the time students, especially seniors, leave for lunch. I don't want to go, but I'm still hungry, even though I've already eaten the lunch Jenny packed. I give him my order: a couple of carne asada tacos.

I'm looking forward to time by myself, actually. Since being back at school, everyone seems concerned about my reentry. From teachers to students, it's as if everyone got the same memo:

Mark Santos is returning to school after the traumatic loss of his twin, Grace. Please don't mention Grace when you're with him, except to express how sorry you are, and then move on. Please make sure Mark is not left alone during the day. Be positive when you're around him.

It's making me a little jittery.

I avoid everyone by looking down and keeping my earbuds in, though I don't even have any music on. In the hallway, I pass a couple of guitarists sitting on the ground, playing dueling versions of "Stairway to Heaven." I give them the nod and keep walking.

I only have one more year and after that, who knows. The cutoff for early admissions to Berklee College of Music is November 1, and I'm not going to make that. I think the next deadline is mid-January, so I still have some time if I want to try to go in the fall. Dad stopped bugging me about it when I started seeing Chris. I think they both felt it was placing too much pressure on me, but my music advisor keeps asking me about my plans. She's trying not to push, but I know she wants me to be proactive. She's worried that I'll miss my window of opportunity. Who says I have to go to school right away? I'm not sure I want to be in some professional orchestra. I could take the studio musician track. Maybe I could hook up with some artist and go on tour for a year or two. Everything's uncertain now.

I hear the music and the dancers laughing and yelling before I round the corner of the hallway. Dancers. They have no problem expressing exactly how they feel all the time and they're always hugging or touching each other. At the moment, half of them have some kind of massage train going where they're rubbing the person's back in front of them. The other half has got a dance circle going.

They ignore my attempt to be invisible and some girl pulls me into the middle of their circle. I try to get away, but more girls surround me and start shaking their bodies up against me. Normally this might not be a bad thing, but I'm just trying to get some space. I spot Levon in the group.

"Levon? Help!"

He smiles and jumps in with some amazing B-boy moves, a total distraction, allowing me to get away.

"Thanks, man!" I yell, backing away.

There are two places people go on campus besides the quad and classrooms: the basement and the roof. Both are utilized for two things—ditching class and making out. The teachers know this, of course, as half of them graduated from the school. As long as we're cool about it, they're cool and don't hassle us. They know we need a place to let off some steam. I'm not doing either. I just need to get some air.

On top of the building, I'm glad to see that I'm alone. I turn around, giving myself a panoramic view of downtown LA, the valley, and the mountains. It rained a little yesterday, so the city has been washed clean of its usual smog and you can actually see the horizon. Some people complain about LA. It's crowded. It's the kind of place that'll crush your dreams rather than make them. It's fake. But from where I'm standing, all I see is potential. All different kinds of people are smashed up against each other, which makes living here more interesting. LA's got everything you could want within driving distance. You've just got to find a way to get there.

I walk to the edge of the roof. Below me is the concrete sidewalk that connects this building to the others. The building's not very high up, only three stories. Leaning over, I wonder if I'd walk away from the fall. I'd probably break my leg. Painful. Pointless. If I were going to jump, I'd want it to matter.

"There was this guy who did it at my old school last year," a voice says behind me.

I turn sharply. Near the metal air-cooling system, Brandon's taking out his cello from its case. *How did he get up here without me hearing him?* "Did what?"

"Jumped. In the middle of the day, when we were changing classes."

I stare at him, wondering what he's getting at. Is he saying this because he thinks I might do it? Because he's thought about it? I size him up. White kid. A sophomore. Not too tall, but not short either. I probably only have two inches on him. Black nails. Eyeliner. Looks like he's going for early glam rock/punk, more Ramones than Autistic Youth. I remember when Brandon transferred last year. He's a good musician. This year we're in orchestra together, but we've never really had a conversation.

"His head cracked open," he continues. "Sounded kind of like a watermelon splitting. That's what they use for the sound effects in zombie movies, you know. My uncle works in the industry. The school cleaned everything up, but . . . blood stains."

"Yeah," I say, and back away from the edge. "Blood, it stains."

"Name was Ryan."

Then I get it. "Were you friends with him?"

"Bingo."

"Sorry."

Brandon places the cello between his legs. "You never know what a person is going through. Ryan seemed like he was fine, and then I guess he wasn't." He holds his bow over the strings and begins to play warm, deep notes.

"Have you thought about it?"

He shrugs. "Everyone thinks about it sometime, but only the insane do it. No offense, man."

"I don't think about it," I lie. I don't as much as I used to.

The more time passes, the more my self-preservation instinct seems to have kicked in.

Brandon continues to play. I look out at the skyscrapers in the distance and wonder why I've never brought my bass up here. Brandon shifts now to Bach, one of the pieces we're working on in class.

"Sebastian played me a new track this morning and it's pretty sick," I say. "Thought I might lay some bass over it. Cello would be a nice touch."

As if on cue, the door to the stairs opens and Sebastian and Pete burst through.

"Told you he'd be here," Pete says. "Santos, we've got your food."

He places a white paper bag in my hands. "Thanks." I pull out one of the tacos, unwrap the foil, and take a bite. So cheap. So simple. So good.

"Hey, Brandon," Sebastian says.

"Hey." He stops playing.

"I'm Pete." Pete holds out his hand to Brandon. They shake.

"Brandon."

"What're you doing?" Sebastian asks.

"Just messing around," Brandon says. "Mark says you've been working on some new beats?"

"Yeah."

"Beats? What beats?" Pete asks.

Sebastian pulls out his phone and lets us listen to what he played me this morning. Brandon starts to softly play along, and I can hear the beginnings of a piece.

"You could add the cello," Brandon says to me as if he hears what I'm composing in my head.

I nod. "Cello, bass, beats."

Sebastian, Brandon, and I keep listening to the track, moving our heads to the music.

"I have an idea," Pete says. His eyes are all lit up and huge. "It'll be perfect. You know how I'm doing a fashion show, right?"

We all give him a blank look.

"Seriously? It's for my senior thesis. I'm getting a big block of time during the winter talent show."

The talent show at our school is a big deal. It's not some free-for-all where you're embarrassed for the people on the stage. Students really get to shine. Sure, there are recitals and concerts and plays that each artistic discipline puts on throughout the year, but the talent show is strictly run by students, and there are serious auditions. It sells out every year, so it's also a major fundraiser for the school.

"You three are going to supply the music," Pete says.

Sebastian and Brandon keep nodding their heads. "Cool," they both say.

I don't know if I want to be roped into one of Pete's performances. There's the time factor, along with having to engage with others. "I don't know, Pete. I'm kind of busy. We have orchestra and jazz band performances."

"You always have those," he says. "This'll be your chance to stop lurking around, avoiding most of humanity. It's senior year. We'll make history with this performance."

"I'm not lurking," I say, but realize I'm sulking when I say it, so I straighten up.

Pete's pushing is beginning to piss me off. I don't like to be pushed. I look at Sebastian for help.

He shrugs and says, "It might be a good idea. Orchestra's no big deal this semester. It'll get your mind off of . . . I mean, on this year."

I know he means to say, *Get your mind off of Grace*, but I'm glad he doesn't because I might have to punch him in the nose. I don't know what's happening, how everything is about doing the talent show. I'm now feeling claustrophobic on the rooftop. I eye the door and think about making a break for it.

"I was having trouble coming up with a theme, but this is perfect." Pete walks along the side of the roof like he's balancing on a tight rope. "I'll get Krysta to work on a downtown skyline for the sets. We'll have models, dancers, musicians, dancers as models. . . . Sebastian and Mark, you guys can handle the music. Maybe it could count for your senior thesis as well. It'll be huge."

Brandon, Sebastian, and Pete are all looking at me. I want to tell them no. I want to tell them to leave so I can be alone. I just want to slip through the school year without drawing attention. Getting pulled into Pete's fashion-show drama—and it's Pete, so I know it'll be drama—is the last thing I want to do. But I've never said no to Pete, and when I don't say anything, Pete takes that as a yes.

"Great. When do you think you'll have something ready?"

Eleven

've parked across the street from the small yellow house. I watch the front door and wait—for what, I'm not sure. It's not like I'm going to get out of the car and walk over. I've played that scene over in my head many times and it never ends well. Watching this house has become one of my routines, like my trips to the bridge. I park in the same spot each time. I'm a little surprised that no one's noticed and called the cops.

I take out my phone and post a question for anyone who's online at Twinless Twins.

Am I still considered a twin?

It only takes a couple of moments for the answers to come.

Kelly: Yes.

Brian: Yes.

Greg: Yes.

Susan: Yes.

John: Yes.

Greg: You'll always be Grace's twin. Death doesn't end that.

Kelly: Once a twin, always a twin.

Brian: Brady and Brian. Brian and Brady. It's been ten years and I still link his name with mine in my head.

I do the same thing. I don't say it out loud, but I still think in terms of we: Grace and me. A unit. One *we* instead of two singular *I*s.

Susan: Forever

I look up from my phone. Across the street, a few kids are now running around the front yard. They don't even look old enough for elementary school. Their mom sits on the front porch, talking on her phone, watching them. She's pretty, even from this distance.

The dad comes out with a soccer ball. He drops it on the ground and kicks it to the older one in the red shirt. He tries to kick it back, but misses. He runs and grabs the ball with his hands instead and pushes it to his dad.

The dad smiles and shows the two boys how to kick the ball. They don't really get it; they're too young to play soccer. But the dad is patient and keeps at it. I can't hear him, but I imagine he's saying *Good job*, over and over again.

After a few passes, the younger boy wraps his arms around his dad's legs. The dad staggers backward, as if the kid's strength is pushing him. The older boy jumps on his dad. This time the dad falls to the ground with both boys on top of him. They wrestle and roll around in the grass. Even though my windows are up, I can hear their squeals.

I remember when Grace and I would do that with Dad. We had a game where we'd get points for pinning different parts of Dad's body to the ground. One point for each finger. Five points for a hand or an elbow. Ten points for a leg. Twenty for his head. If we could get his whole body down, that was an automatic victory. It always took the two of us to do it. Grace had a trick that worked most of the time. She'd distract Dad, pretending to get hurt. I knew she was faking because she'd smile out of the left side of her mouth. While Dad was checking her arm or whatever she'd said she'd injured, I'd pounce and she'd jump and we'd take Dad by surprise. Watching this father play with his sons, I'm wondering if Dad knew and just played along. There was no way we'd actually have been able to tackle a grown man at six.

The dad is on his back now with his boys sitting on his stomach and chest. They look happy. And their joy shines a spotlight on my own unhappiness. It's not fair. My hands grip the steering wheel. I think about getting out of the car, but I hadn't figured kids into the equation. Not that I really had much of a plan to begin with. I don't even know what I would say to the guy.

I watch the family through the car window like they're characters in a silent movie. Eventually I start the engine and pull away from the curb, taking my memories of when my family seemed that happy with me.

Twelve

anna, Sebastian, and I meet at a yogurt place to map out a tentative plan for completing Grace's list. The start of the school year had proved busier than we thought, especially for Hanna. We've been training together, but we haven't technically done anything on Grace's list yet. Hanna's freaking out about accomplishing everything in time.

After thirty minutes of discussion, we have a plan. We're starting this weekend with surfing, which takes care of September. Bungee jumping will be in October, with spoken word and hiking in November. The 5K will be last. Hanna has already signed us up for one on December 28. It's pushing our deadline, but everything will be done before the year is over.

Hanna writes the plan down on a small napkin and passes it for me to see. I can't pick it up. My hands are suddenly immovable weights. I knew this was what we were doing, what I agreed to, but I'm not prepared for how I feel. What'll happen when we're finished? Will I be cured of missing her? Will I feel more lonely than before?

"Sebastian," Hanna says, "you've got some chocolate on your mouth."

He grabs the napkin with our schedule and wipes it off.

"Sebastian!" Hanna cries.

He smoothes out the napkin on the table. "Sorry."

I watch the four guys hunched over individual gaming systems at a table in the middle of the shop. They're playing something together, even though they aren't talking and there's no physical interaction. There's a group of gamers at my school who do the same thing every lunch, totally oblivious to everyone around them.

"Well, man," Sebastian says, "what do you think? Doable?"

I know they want me to tell them that it's all good, that seeing Grace's last wishes laid out on a chocolate-smudged napkin is perfectly normal, and that I'm okay with it. But it feels like some vacation itinerary.

I want to say I've changed my mind, but I say, "Fine. It's fine." I don't want to disappoint them. I finish my yogurt in one last bite.

"Great!" Hanna pushes her yogurt across the table. "Have mine. I can't eat it all."

I take a bite and grimace. "What's this?" I almost gag.

"You like it?" Hanna asks. Her eyes sparkle mischievously.

"It's disgusting." I stand up and get a cup of water to wash away the taste of her strawberry-and-raspberry concoction. Hanna knows I don't like berries, except for blueberries. I could eat a basketful of blueberries anytime.

"It is not!" she calls after me.

"You did that on purpose."

She tilts her head and says, "Maybe," playfully. I sit back down.

"It can't be that bad," Sebastian says. He takes a bite. "A little on the sweet side."

He and Hanna talk dessert, while I finish off my water. It's weird to have Sebastian and Hanna together, especially here. This was a place the three of us, Hanna, Grace, and I, would go all the time. But we usually sat where the gamers are. Sebastian is probably my best friend, but he can't replace Grace, not that he's trying. He's telling a joke about the alien who doesn't know he's an alien, and even though I've heard it before, I laugh with Hanna as if it's the first time.

Jenny gets word that we're going surfing tomorrow morning. I don't tell her why. I'm not sure what she and Dad would think about Grace's list. Maybe they'd ask to come with us, but I want to keep it between Hanna, Sebastian, and me. I don't want it getting out of hand. Jenny gets all excited and rents a movie. She says there's a scene about learning how to surf that'll be good for me. I don't want to watch it alone, so I invite Sebastian and Hanna to come for dinner and a movie. I beg, actually, and they do.

"You're going to love *Point Break*. It used to be my favorite back in the day. I can't believe it's more than twenty years old already." Jenny laughs nervously. "I'm so old."

"Jenny, you are not old," Hanna says.

"Thank you, Hanna. Ready?" she calls for my dad.

"Coming!" he says, and enters with a bowl of M&M's that he places alongside the popcorn and bottled waters on the coffee table. He sits next to Jenny on the love seat. Dad indulges Jenny with movie nights, but I know he would prefer hiding away and reading the new crime novel he checked out at the library.

Hanna sits in between Sebastian and me. She scoots toward me to give Sebastian more room.

Hanna whispers, "Jenny's so cute."

"No matter what, just tell her you like it," I whisper back, very aware that our sides are practically glued together. Hanna doesn't seem to notice. She acts like we always sit like this for

Friday night movies at my house. She's been to plenty of them, but we've never sat this close. She stares at the screen. I cross my arms, uncertain of where to place them.

Friday-night movies are kind of a tradition. It started when we were kids. Grace and I used to take turns deciding what movie to see. That was usually fine because we had similar taste. Grace loved action and scary movies, and I didn't mind an occasional chick flick. She also loved old musicals, especially the ones with Gene Kelly. The last movie we watched together was *An American in Paris*. She wanted to go to Paris one day. That would've probably made another list: Top Five Cities to Visit Before I Die.

Point Break is actually pretty cool. Lots of action and humor, and a sex scene, which was only awkward because my parents were in the room. All of the skydiving makes me wish that had been on Grace's list. The main chase scene is awesome. Two guys run through alleys and houses, and the camera is all shaky, like we're there with them. One of them even throws a pit bull as a distraction. I'd never seen that before.

After the credits roll, we discuss the probability of Johnny Utah catching Bodhi in the part when he jumps from the plane without a parachute. In the movie he grabs him while they're free-falling. Sebastian and I want to know if that could really happen.

"It could happen," Jenny says, as if she really believes it.

"The guy has only been skydiving once and suddenly he knows how to expertly maneuver himself in the air? Not possible," Sebastian says, and he starts looking something up on his phone.

"It's a movie," my dad says. "None of it's real. They probably filmed it in a studio with wind machines." He stands up and stretches before clearing the coffee table.

"Boo," Jenny says. "You guys have no imagination."

"You didn't like the movie, Mr. Santos?" Hanna asks.

"It's called *amore*," he says, and kisses Jenny on the cheek before taking the empty bowl to the kitchen.

"Cute," Hanna says. Cute except when it's your own parents. I continue our discussion of the movie.

"Also, how long has he known the girl? Like two weeks? He's willing to jump out of a plane for her?" I say.

Jenny and Hanna both look at me with wide-eyed shock.

"Of course he is," Hanna says. "They have a *connection*."

"Meaning she has blue eyes and a decent body," I say about the girl.

"It's more than just physical. Besides, it's Keanu Reeves," Hanna says.

"What does that mean?

"He's hot."

"I know, right?" Jenny says, and they laugh.

"Ha!" Sebastian says, his face still in his phone. "Technically you *could* jump like that, but the timing is off in the film. You can't free-fall for as long as they did. And they wouldn't be able to hear each other over the wind. So no talking, either. Told you!" He looks up triumphantly.

I smile, but Jenny and Hanna just stare at Sebastian as if he's dropped their birthday cake all over the floor.

Jenny points at his phone. "And this is the problem with technology. It kills the illusion." She sighs. "Well, be careful out there tomorrow," Jenny says. "You've seen how those surfers can get."

"Jenny, it's just a movie. We're going with Charlie. He knows the scene," I say, but I don't want to be rude, so I add, "But thank you. I feel like I could probably surf right now."

"Yeah. We could probably do a mean pop-up." To show her, Sebastian jumps up from the couch into the surfer's stance.

"No, Sebastian, it's more like this." I demonstrate the move from the floor, wobbling back and forth as if I'm on a board.

"All right. All right. I get it. Good night, guys. Make sure you lock up, Mark." She heads upstairs.

"Are we seriously going surfing tomorrow?" Hanna asks. "I don't think I can do it."

"We probably won't get up on the board, but yes," Sebastian says. "Where are you putting me tonight?" Sebastian is staying over so we can all drive together.

"My room. Floor."

"I'm going to go," Hanna says, and pushes up off the couch. "If Charlie's serious about when we're meeting, I need my sleep."

"When it comes to surfing, Charlie's serious," Sebastian says.

I walk Hanna to the door.

"Bye, Sebastian," she says, and waves.

"Later."

Hanna pauses at the door. "You really don't think someone would jump out of a plane to save a girl?"

I shrug. "Call me a realist."

"Even if he loved her?"

"That kind of love takes years," I say. "It doesn't happen in a couple hours."

She smiles like I've said the right thing.

"See you later," she says.

"I'll send you a wake-up text at five thirty."

She groans as the screen door closes behind her. I watch her walk down the steps, across the street, and open her front door before I close mine.

Sebastian gives me a look.

"What?"

"Nothing," he says, but he smirks.

"We're just friends."

"Sure, whatever you say. She didn't scooch up next to *me* on that couch."

"Hanna's practically another sister." I start climbing the stairs.

Sebastian makes a tinny noise and I look at him. He's rubbing two fingers together on his right hand. "My tiny violin's playing sad music for you."

"Shut up." I turn on the light in my room.

"Maybe I'll take a crack at her, then."

I throw a pillow at his head and that shuts him up. Sebastian could ask Hanna out, I guess. It's not like she's seeing anyone, at least I don't think she is. But the idea of Hanna dating someone, even Sebastian, doesn't sit well with me.

I think of the way we sat together on the couch, our bodies pressed together as if it were normal. I let my mind linger and imagine if I had wrapped my arm around her, pulling her closer. But I stop myself. I wonder what Hanna thinks.

All night I toss and turn. I dream I'm skydiving. Hanna is free-falling with me. We're holding hands and she's smiling. Her hair's all wild and I can't see her eyes well through the bug-like goggles she's wearing. She shouts something, but I can't hear her.

"What?" I yell.

"Are you ready?" she asks.

"For what?"

She laughs and lets go of my hands. I try to grab hold of her, but she pulls on her chute. It pops open, and she rips away from me. I go to pull mine, but I can't get my parachute to open. I tug frantically on the string, but it won't work. The ground is coming faster and faster. I hear Hanna calling my name just as I'm about to hit the pavement, and I wake up.

My heart is racing. From the sleeping bag, Sebastian snores. I try to go back to sleep, but I can't. I keep seeing Hanna's body floating farther and farther away from me, even with my eyes wide open.

Thirteen

Early next morning we're at El Porto just outside of Manhattan Beach. The oil refinery's stacks blow gray smoke, adding to the already cloudy sky. It doesn't seem like the perfect day for surfing, but a handful of surfers are already in the water, out past the break. The volleyball nets are empty. A lifeguard wearing an orange Windbreaker sits perched on top of his tower.

Charlie runs out of the ocean, board at his side. He places it on the sand and shakes his head back and forth, whipping the water from his blond hair in our direction.

Hanna squeals when some of the droplets hit her. "It's cold!"

"Great day for the water, folks," Charlie says. He's wearing his wet suit and looks exactly how you'd expect a California surfer to look, which is kind of funny because he's from Kansas. Out of the four of us, Sebastian and I are the only true Angelenos; Hanna is originally from Seattle.

"Why don't you guys get in your suits? Here's yours," Charlie says, handing one to Sebastian.

Sebastian, Hanna, and I drop our clothes in a pile on the blanket. Hanna's wearing a white swim shirt and bikini bottoms. I notice Pepe is covered in some kind of casing, probably to protect it from getting wet, but I don't draw attention to it. She doesn't hide the fact that she has diabetes, but she doesn't go and advertise it to everyone either.

She reaches for her wet suit and steps into it, jumping a little to try and pull it on. She does this quickly and self-consciously. Hanna's always thinking she has a big butt. I guess I contributed to that, telling her she did when we were kids. I notice Charlie and Sebastian peek at her when they think she's not looking. She has no idea how they see her, and I can tell you they do not mind her butt at all.

I reach behind me and pull up my suit's zipper. Hanna has some trouble with hers.

"Here. Turn around," I tell her. I take the zipper at the base of her spine and zip her up tight.

"Thanks," she says, and turns to face me. She touches my chest. "You look good in a wet suit, Mark."

"Not bad yourself." She looks amazing.

"Yeah, right." She puts her hands on her hips and smiles up at me. "I don't even have on makeup."

"You never need makeup."

"Let's warm up." Charlie's voice interrupts the moment. At least I *think* we're having a moment. At his words Hanna snaps to attention and steps away from me. "The water's cold, and cold muscles equal injuries."

I notice Sebastian and burst out laughing. The suit is way too big for him, baggy instead of tight, and he's had to roll the bottoms. Charlie is, like, double the size of Sebastian.

"Shut up," he says, and tries to smooth out some of the suit.

Charlie laughs too. "Sorry, man. It's all I had. It should still keep you warm."

Charlie leads us through a series of stretches, much like the ones Hanna and I do before we run, although that's tapered off a bit. At first we were running every morning before school; now we do it Mondays and Wednesdays. I run on the weekends, but I go alone. I wouldn't have thought I'd actually like running, but I do.

Charlie has brought two boards for us to use. He lies down on one of them. "Now I'm going to show you how to do a basic pop-up."

At the word "pop-up," Sebastian and I laugh, remembering the movie and how we teased Jenny.

Charlie continues, "Will you be doing this today? Maybe not, but we're going to try."

It feels good to be here at the beach with friends. I can't remember the last time I was at the ocean. I pretend we're just learning to surf, nothing more.

Charlie has us practice when he's done demonstrating. Sebastian gives me his board when he's done. It's not as easy as Charlie made it look. Though since I skate, I understand where my feet should go, how to balance. But this is on land. I have no idea how I'll do in the water.

"We won't be going too deep," Charlie says. "We'll work with the white-water waves, ones that have already broken. Last tip: When catching a wave, look for the one with a little distance. When you feel the wave start to give you that extra push, keep paddling, like, three extra strokes, and then try to pop up. Let's go."

Basically Charlie's philosophy is to let us flop around and mess up like a bunch of kooks, which is exactly what we are, since none of us has surfed before. I don't know why I haven't learned. It's a Southern California rite of passage that I've just never cared about. I'm surprised Grace did.

My feet touch the water and it's freezing. I jump up and down a couple of times and then rush in. I'd seen other surfers doing that, pointing the nose of their boards into the water, diving and rising like a dolphin, which is what I pictured doing.

Not quite. For me, there's a lot of splashing and I kind of belly flop on the board and slide off.

I look back at the shore. Hanna is timidly working her way in, while Sebastian sits this one out. Charlie stands with Hanna, which is fine. She'll probably need more help. I notice that Charlie's hands are all over Hanna, which is not fine. It's like I'm watching some stupid romantic comedy where the guy teaches the girl how to play pool by coming up behind her to help her hold a cue. Hanna giggles and Charlie steadies her on the board.

Oh, please, Hanna. Like you can't get on a board. She's acting like she's helpless, and I hate when she does that. Even though I did just fall off myself. I wasn't putting on a show. I focus on what I'm doing instead of what's going on with Hanna. I'm not here for her.

I paddle out. It's rough, trying to paddle and stay on the board. I tighten my core and work to keep my balance centered. I see a wave and have to get off to turn the board around. I try to remember what Charlie said about waiting until the wave pushes you.

The wave hits the board and I push myself up, but the board starts to tip. I have to grab on to the rails to steady myself, but the force of the wave hits and shoots the board out from underneath me. I'm pulled under. It tugs at the leash around my ankle. I surface and swim to the board, grab it, and get back on. It's much harder than I thought, but I need to do this. Number five on Grace's list said to surf, not to fall and splash around in the ocean.

Another wave heads toward me. I try again with pretty much the same results. To get more of a feel for the board and the waves, I catch a few using the surfboard like a boogie board, but I still flop around. After what feels like hours of getting pummeled, I finally get a break. The wave carries me and I push up, not jumping to my feet, but using a knee to thrust me upward. It works. I'm actually standing on the board. I'm all wobbly because I can't get my balance. I hold out my arms to try and steady myself, but I flip backward, crashing into the white water. I jump up because I'm now where I can stand and whip the water out of my face. For a few seconds I was actually surfing. Charlie and Hanna are cheering. Sebastian yells something from the shore, but I can't hear him over the ocean.

Determined now, I catch a couple more waves in the white water, trying to feel how to maneuver, trying to get a sense of balance and board and motion. After probably ten waves, I find one that I can stand up on again. I'm still shaky, but this time the ride lasts for maybe ten seconds instead of five.

I take the board just past where the waves are breaking. Not that they're huge waves or anything. It's pretty tame here, and there's a sandbar, so it's not that deep. I run both hands through my hair to smooth it out. The water's cold on my face and hands, but I'm warm, protected by the suit.

I see Hanna's out of the water now, and Sebastian is on the

board. The first wave slams him. I laugh out loud, wondering if I looked that ridiculous. Probably.

I glanced at the smokestacks. It's not what you'd think of as picturesque. The water's cloudy, probably from the refinery. A plane flies overhead, a reminder of how close we are to the Los Angeles airport. Charlie said this was a good place to learn, though. The locals are friendly and expect beginners. There's a cluster of surfers nearby who don't seem to mind me flailing around. I've tried to steer as far clear of them as I can. The clouds are starting to break overhead and sunlight hits the top of the waves.

"So, Grace," I say. "Here we are. What do you think?"

Grace hated the cold. She hated getting wet. She hated the water. Whenever we went to the beach, which wasn't really that much, she stayed on the shore, collecting the small sand crabs. When the water came in, they'd get flooded out of their holes. When the water was drawn back into the ocean, the crabs would try to bury themselves quickly before the next wave came. They'd make these V-shaped lines in the sand. That's how you knew where to dig for them. She'd run and scoop the sand, then she'd hold her hand over a bucket and let the crabs fall inside. I did it with her, but I didn't like the way it felt when they tried to dig into your hands. It didn't hurt, but it kind of freaked me out, like they were little alien creatures burrowing into my skin.

Grace's wish list is odd. It's very physical, and all things she hadn't done before. In fact, it seems more like things she was *afraid* of doing. Why would Grace have wanted to surf? Did she secretly like the water? Did someone else put her up to it? Did River? He didn't seem the surfing type.

Thinking of River gives me a headache, like one of those behind-the-eye headaches that takes coffee, Excedrin, a shower, and going to bed to finally get rid of it. I don't get migraines very often: the first time was last year after a very stressful week of tests, practice, a recital, and jazz band concert. The second time was after the accident.

I see a wave coming in, shake my head free of River, and decide to go for it. It'll be a big one because it's on the outside of the break, but I'm ready. I turn and wait for the water to start to take me. I paddle hard and when it starts propelling me forward, I push up. This time I pop up to my feet, without using my knees. But I don't anticipate the force of the wave dropping, and I'm thrown off the board and crash underneath the water. I try to swim, to get to the surface, but I'm caught in the churning water. I panic. The undertow spins me around, and I'm confused about which way is up. I don't know how long I've been under, but it feels like a long time. My chest begins to hurt because I'm still holding my breath. I try to relax, thinking that maybe if I do, I'll float to the surface. I'm suddenly very calm.

I wonder if this is how Grace felt at the end. If there was a moment of peace right after she said my name and the car hit us. Right before she stopped breathing, did she have a brief moment when dying came as naturally as living?

My brain feels like it's going to explode, and my reflexes take over. My body wants to live. I break through the surface, gulping a huge breath. I cough and cough from all the water I hadn't even realized I'd swallowed.

"Mark!" I hear my name being called. Charlie is near me. "Can you get on your board?"

"Yeah," I shout between gasps. Surprisingly, my board is still attached to my ankle.

"Get on it. Follow me in."

I'm right where the waves are breaking, and another one is coming quickly. I get on my board and paddle in, staying close to Charlie.

At the shore, I stumble out of the water, dragging my board. I'm a little shaky. Charlie pats me on the back.

"Awesome, bro. Fearless." He laughs.

"Are you okay?" Hanna asks as soon as I reach the blanket. She hands me my towel.

"Yeah," I say, still out of breath.

"I was so scared. It took forever for you to come up." She hits me. "Don't do that again!"

"Like I planned that." I am relieved to be back on shore.

"How'd it go?" I ask Sebastian.

"Not in my DNA."

"I got on one knee," Hanna says, all proud of herself.

"You guys were great," Charlie says. He looks out at the ocean. "A good set's coming in. Mind if I get in a few before we go?"

"Have at it," Sebastian says.

The three of us sit on the blanket watching the water, while Charlie heads out. He makes it look easy, as do the other surfers out there. We watch him take a wave, riding it much longer than I ever did. When he's finished, he just floats over the lip of the wave and sits on the board to wait for another one.

"He's really good," Hanna says. She takes a CapriSun out of the bag she brought with her. It takes her a couple of tries to puncture the straw through.

"I had no idea how hard this was," Sebastian says. "I'll stick to land."

"You think you'll do it again?" I ask Hanna.

"Maybe," Hanna says. "Charlie's a good teacher. But my arms are going to be crazy sore tomorrow."

It did take a lot of upper-body strength with all that paddling. I don't admit it, but I know I'm going to be sore tomorrow too.

"I can't believe it's only nine a.m. On a Saturday. I should still be sleeping," she says.

"I should be prepping food," Sebastian says. He unzips the suit and lies back against his towel.

Charlie wipes out on a big wave. "Ouch," I say. But he gets right back up on the board and paddles out again.

"Grace would have . . . ," Hanna begins, and stops.

I finish her thought. "Hated this."

Hanna laughs. "I know! What was she thinking? She barely liked it when we'd go swimming and play Marco Polo at the community pool when we were kids."

"I'd always give her position away."

"Yeah, 'cause you were a cheater," Hanna says.

"I'd win the splash wars, even with the two of you ganging up on me," I say.

"You were such a brat."

We're both quiet, remembering our summers at the pool.

"It's a list of fears," I say finally. "They are things she was afraid of doing."

"Maybe we should say something. Recognize the moment," Hanna says.

I know she's waiting for me to initiate, but I can't. Besides, this was all Hanna's idea. I watch Charlie catch another wave. It's beautiful and simple. He rides for maybe twenty seconds and then gets off, to wait for another.

I think about how the ocean never stops. It's relentless. It keeps going forever and ever. I pick up a handful of sand and let it fall through my fingers. I wonder how long it took for the beach to be made. How many years for the ocean to beat against stone and rock, until they crumbled. What can I say about Grace?

A small stone remains in my palm. It's smooth and dark, standing out from the pale grains. I don't want to be a pebble turning into sand, rubbed free of Grace. I want to keep her in my heart and hold her deep, where the waters cannot touch.

"Grace, if you're watching us. We miss you and love you," Hanna says, since I'm not giving her any help. "Thanks for getting us to surf. And may we never do it again." She smiles.

"Right on," Sebastian says.

I stand and walk down to the water's edge. I throw the stone into the ocean. As the surf retreats, I spot the V tracks, like tiny clusters of birds flying in formation, in the wet sand. I bend down and dig. I hold a huge clump of sand and watch the tiny crabs thrash. They reach the palm of my hand, but I don't release them. They try to claw into my skin, but their limbs aren't strong enough. I want to feel the pain of them cutting through, but all I feel is an irritating rubbing, like time itself pressing against earth and ocean. I tilt my palm and they drop into the sand, disappearing.

Suddenly there's a foot with orange toenails digging right in the spot where I've dropped the crabs.

"Gross," Hanna says.

I get up. "You're probably killing them with your big feet."

"Oh no you didn't," she says.

"What?"

"Say I have big feet."

"Well, they're big to the crabs."

She skips to the water and splashes me with her foot. I look at her. Her eyes are dancing. She tries to dart away, but I catch her in the middle and pick her up.

"No!" she shrieks. "Mark, put me down!"

Even though she's kicking and squirming, I carry her into the water and throw her into a wave. But I stumble and fall as I do it. Then she's on top of me, climbing on my back, trying to take me down.

"You are so dead!" she shouts. Another wave crashes into us and we both go under. She comes up coughing.

"You okay?" I ask, and reach for her, pulling her away from the deeper waters, to where she can stand. This time she comes willingly.

"Yes. I just need to catch my breath."

I hold her, waiting until she tells me she's okay. Instead she slips her arm around my waist while the waves break against us again and again.

Fourteen

On Sunday morning I sleep in while everyone goes to church. I stopped going right after Grace died. My parents didn't make me, and I am grateful for it. I overheard Dad telling Jenny a while back that "He'll come when he's ready." I don't tell them that I may never be ready.

Church is not a bad place. I used to play for the band, and Marty, the band's leader, still sends me an e-mail or text from time to time about coming to practice. Good bass players are always hard to find. But I don't know if I can be in a room with God and all those people who've known Grace and me for years. I think I'd suffocate. I don't want them asking me how I'm doing, or telling me how much they loved Grace. I don't want their kindness. Their kindness kills me. It's not the sugary-sweet kind. It's genuine and motivated by love and there's no fighting it. Sometimes love can be more overwhelming than hate. So I don't go.

I pull a pair of jeans out of my drawer and throw on a T-shirt before heading downstairs. There's a yellow sticky note for me on the fridge in Jenny's handwriting. *Mark, call your mom.* I crumple it up and throw it in the trash. They can't make me talk to her. Where was she before Grace died? She had years to reach out. *Years.* I'm not going to be the one to hold her hand through this.

I open the front door and stand outside. I should get in some bass practice, but I'm tempted to head over to Hanna's. I hesitate though. After the beach, it's like something's shifted. I remember how her skin felt against mine as I held her in the ocean. It would be so much easier if Grace were here. She'd tell me what to do, although I know what she'd probably say.

Grace told me once that Hanna and I just needed to get it over with. Make out or something already. I'd ask her what Hanna thought about me, but like I said, Grace was always the best at keeping secrets. She said I was being stubborn by not admitting my own feelings.

You can't make out with one of your best friends. Life isn't like a movie. Friends with benefits never work. Someone always gets hurt. Hanna and I have a good thing going. I don't want to screw it up, not that I don't imagine what it'd be like to kiss her.

Now that Grace isn't here as our buffer, every time I'm with Hanna I'm a little more on edge, hyperaware of her presence. She's always been beautiful, but it's like I've finally woken up and am seeing her from a different angle. Like how funny she is. How she's willing to try new things. How cool she was with Sebastian, as if she's known him forever. How she checks up on me without making it seem as if she is. How she makes me feel that things are going to be okay.

Besides, since losing Grace, I don't know how I'd deal with losing Hanna, too. What if she doesn't have feelings for me? It's not worth the risk.

I find myself at her front door and knock. Her mom answers.

"Hello, Mark. Come on in. They're in the back."

"Thanks, I'll just go around." *They're?*

"Suit yourself." She closes the door.

I open the side gate and head for the yard. I see Hanna and River as soon as I round the corner of the house. They're on the swing, heads bent together as if, well, I don't want to think about what they're doing. I turn and leave.

I'm starting to cross the street when I hear my name.

"Mark, wait." It's Hanna. "Where you going?"

"Nowhere. A drive."

"Why don't you stay?"

"I'm good." I turn my back to her. Hanna stops in the middle of the street, but I keep walking.

"You can't run forever," she calls.

She's wrong. You *can* run forever—or at least for a long time. I get in Dad's car and Charlie Mingus plays from a CD. I'm already feeling better. I can always count on Dad to have killer music.

Sometimes I go down to the coast, but since I was just there, I take the 5 and head north. I want some space. Cars scatter across four lanes of freeway. I'm practically alone. I let the jazz carry me onward. I pass Magic Mountain with its huge roller coasters and wonder why I never go. It's not that far. I keep driving, not really having a destination in mind.

I feel something sharp in my pocket. I pull out Grace's bracelet, the one that was in the package from the police department, and turn it over in my hand. I had forgotten I'd stuffed it in my pocket that day. The bracelet is delicate and shiny, like new.

Grace met River at the beginning of junior year. She hid him from us at first, but that was just like Grace. She was incredibly private, especially about the guys in her life, not that she dated a lot or had many boyfriends. She was picky. She said things like, "Dating someone isn't like trying on clothes. It's got to mean something to hold someone's hand or let a guy kiss you. At least, it *should* mean something. I don't need fireworks when I'm with him, but I want him to be someone I admire and respect." She was always deep like that. Of course, it'd make me feel all shallow, because I sometimes based my selection on a great pair of legs or a nice chest.

When she brought River over, I was kind of surprised by him. He was this long, angular white guy. Brown hair, totally straight edge. He wore a blue button-down shirt, tucked into his jeans, and a belt when he came for dinner.

He was nervous with me, like he was really trying to make a good impression. He didn't play any instrument. He didn't skate. He was a runner, and I guess pretty good at it. Potential-full-ride-scholarship-for-the-800 good.

Grace had warned me to be nice, so I knew she was serious about him and I cut him a break. I didn't really care who she dated as long as he treated her well, and River seemed to make her happy. I was cool with him, even though we didn't connect.

A couple of months later, Grace pulled me into her room and shut the door.

"What's up?"

"Here," she said, and handed me a small silver bracelet.

"Thank you?" I said.

"It's a bracelet."

I held it out in front of me. "Yep. It's a bracelet."

"River gave it to me last night."

"Looks like your style," I said, and tried to hand it to her, but she backed away.

"I know, right? It's exactly something I'd pick out myself." She paced back and forth.

"And that's a bad thing?"

"I don't know. I don't know what it means," she said, and sat on my bed.

"It's just a bracelet." I tossed it on the bed next to her. She looked at it and didn't pick it up.

"Have you ever given someone a bracelet? One with hearts on it?"

"Well, actually they're more like dewdrops than hearts."

"Mark, seriously."

"Okay, okay. No."

"What's it supposed to mean?"

"He's into you. That's all. Don't overanalyze it."

"But *how* into me? And what, I'm supposed to start wearing it now? Like every day? What if I don't want to wear it? What if I want to change it up, and River sees and gets hurt because I'm not wearing his bracelet?"

"Grace, come on. Stop freaking out."

She fell back on the bed and I lay beside her. From an aerial shot we're obviously not identical, separated by more than a Y chromosome. Her hair is long and layered with bangs. Mine is short, but the same jet-black color and just as straight. I'm also a good head taller than her, but we have the same shape in the eyes and mouth.

"He told me he loved me," Grace says.

It was obvious the guy was totally whipped. He texted her all the time, took her out, came over for Friday movie nights. Now he'd said the three words and given her a present. No wonder Grace was freaking out. "What'd you say?"

"Thank you."

I laughed; I couldn't help it. "Ouch."

"It's not funny, Mark."

"I know, but oh man. What'd he do?"

"He smiled and put his arm around me. What was I supposed to say?"

"I love you too?" I shrugged. I didn't know. I had never told a girl I loved her before. I couldn't believe River had the balls. It kind of made me respect the guy. "Do you love him?"

She was quiet.

"It's okay if you do and it's okay if you don't," I said.

"Maybe I do," she whispered. "Is that weird?"

"Kind of." I patted her on the arm. "But you've always been weird."

"Don't say anything to Dad and Jenny," she said.

"I won't. You going to tell him how you feel?"

"Eventually."

"Make him sweat?"

"Exactly." She sat up, grabbed the bracelet, and put it in her purse. "But not tonight."

A week later we were in the accident.

At the funeral, I played the good son and brother. I was polite, gracious in the onslaught of grief. All of Dad's family came and most of Mom's, along with friends of Grace from school I didn't know. Mom kept trying to touch me, to hold me. I remained impassive.

Everyone said such nice things about Grace. Our pastor shared funny stories. Dad and Jenny spoke. I wanted to speak, but I was afraid I wouldn't be able to keep it together. What they all said about Grace was true, but it was also false. They were only focusing on her good qualities, as if she were this perfect person. Grace was amazing, but she was also human, which meant she was messy and complicated. How could you sum up a person's life in five minutes anyway? It made me feel angry and more detached from her. The person they were all describing wasn't even real.

River came dressed in a black suit and tie. It made him look taller for some reason. He shook my dad's hand and tried to shake Jenny's, but she hugged him. He held on to her for a while. I saw he was crying. When he got to me, his eyes were swollen. We shook hands and he pulled me in for a manly side hug and pat on the back as if he were my uncle, but River wasn't family. He was some guy who'd dated Grace for a couple of months.

At the gravesite, I stayed underneath a tree. I leaned against it as if I were holding it up, but the truth was, it was holding me up. I needed something to keep me together because I was afraid I'd split into pieces. Staring at the casket, I logically knew Grace's body was inside, but my actual Grace wasn't. She was gone. But I felt like she was still with me, I just couldn't see her. How can someone be a living being with dreams and plans, and then suddenly not exist anymore? She didn't even say good-bye.

And I was the one who was supposed to say good-bye. That's what funerals are: a bunch of people coming together to say good-bye to the dead and to face their own mortality. We're all supposed to have a good ugly cry, get the pain out, remember the good times, and then move on. We tell ourselves the dead would want us to do that. We tell ourselves that death is a part of life. We tell ourselves anything to try to make sense of it. One moment Grace was here. The next moment she wasn't. I could find no sense in that.

When they lowered the coffin, I stopped breathing. Just as I had after the accident when I was waiting for her to breathe again. My breath had always kept time with hers. At the gravesite, my chest hurt. My lungs started to burn. I inhaled a huge gulp of oxygen. I would have to learn to breathe on my own.

Then she was in the ground. Gone. Forever. People began peeling away in twos and threes, but I stayed. My back pressed against the tree, as if it'd been nailed to it.

River came up to me.

"Hey."

"Hey."

"I'm sorry," he said, and stood next to me.

That's what everyone kept saying. *I'm sorry. I'm sorry.* Over and over again. No one knew what to say. So instead of just being quiet, they said empty words. Apologies. What were they apologizing for? They weren't the one driving our car. They weren't the one who survived.

Right after we were hit, *I'm sorry* were the first words I heard. I was trying to get out of our car, when the driver who hit us said, "I'm sorry! You okay in there? Oh man. I'm so sorry!"

Grace never got to hear his apology.

He kept saying it over and over, as I crawled out, as I tried to get to Grace, even after the ambulance arrived.

River said it again. "I'm sorry," and all I could hear was that man's voice. A man who'd looked down for a couple of seconds, some teacher, a father of two. He wrote my parents a four-page letter. They actually wrote him back. My dad said without forgiveness a heart would freeze. But I didn't care. I refused to read the letter. Let my heart become Antarctica.

"I loved her, you know. I really did." River's body shook a little.

His confession made me so angry. He didn't love her. He barely knew her. *I* loved her. I felt so possessive, as if no one had the right to miss her like I did. No one could share in that pain.

River put his hand on my shoulder. "If you ever need anything, Mark, I'm here for you."

I shrugged his hand off and pushed him away. Tears rolled down his cheeks as he told me again how sorry he was. I hit him in the face and then in his chest, stomach, wherever I could get in a punch. I'd never hit anyone before. My hands stung with every contact. I heard my dad say my name, but I kept hitting River. He just stood there. He didn't fight back or even hold up his hands to defend himself. Blood trickled from his nose, and he started crying, really crying.

My dad pulled me off of River, holding me from behind. Everyone was there: Jenny, Hanna, my mom, my grandparents, the aunties. Everyone was crying.

"Don't do that!" I yelled at River. "Don't cry for her. She didn't—she didn't even love you!"

"Mark," Dad said. "It's okay. It's okay."

"It's not okay!" I screamed. "It'll never be okay!"

I twisted free of my dad and ran away.

My plan had been to never speak to River again, even though Hanna suggested I make it right. But I couldn't admit my shame at how I had treated River. He hadn't fought back, as if he welcomed the suffering. The pity in his eyes made me hate him. I also hated that he held a piece of Grace I couldn't carry.

The only way the thing between River and me could be made right is if Grace weren't dead. If I could somehow go back in time and not take the bridge or if I could tell the guy not to drive that night.

But you can never go back. You can never undo what you wish you hadn't done. You can't do the things you wish you did.

I'm not sure what I'm going to do with the bracelet. I keep driving, the thin chain cold and heavy in my hand.

Fifteen

Sebastian is better at composing than I am, but he wants me to create the music for Pete's show. He says it's because I'm already hearing a melody. Pete's bugging me about it, even though the show's not until December. I have plenty of time, but I tell him that I'm working on the music during my free period, when I've signed out one of the practice rooms. I've been in here for a good half hour and am starting to lay out parts over Sebastian's track, when there's a knock on the door.

"Come in," I say, irritated that I have to stop.

A Chinese girl with a blue streak through her short black hair stands in the doorway. "Um, Mark?"

"Yeah?"

"Pete told me to come find you."

I look at her like, *Yeah, so what do you want?*

"I'm choreographing for the show. He said you're on music. Is that it?" She's referring to the beats I still have going. I turn off the track.

"Partly. I'll be adding cello and bass."

"Cool. Kind of classical, hip-hop fusion."

"Kind of." I don't recognize her. "What's your name?"

"Lily." She smiles and her whole face lights up. She's cute. "I just transferred in this year. I'm a junior," she says, as if to answer my question about why I haven't seen her before.

Either she's really good or no one wanted to help Pete. I size her up: small frame, skinny, and a little flat in the chest, more like a ballet dancer. She's wearing two-toned black-and-purple leggings, high-top Nike sneakers, and a gray baggy T-shirt with a red flannel tied around her waist.

"I'm supposed to tell you to come to the dance room."

"Now?" I say, a little annoyed because the piece isn't ready.

"Yeah, we're all there."

I think about having her tell Pete I'm not coming, but I know he'll just come here himself and demand my presence. I pack up my bass.

"Where have you been?" Sebastian asks when I follow Lily

into the dance room. He and Brandon are set up in the corner. Pete's talking to someone on his phone.

"No one told me we were having practice."

"Pete said you called it."

"No, I told him I was going to . . . Never mind. Actually, this'll work. I have some ideas we can play around with. Hey, Brandon."

"Hey," he says. "Hi, Lily."

Lily gives him a big smile and sits down on the hardwood floor in front of the mirrors and begins stretching. I talk through what I have in mind with Sebastian and Brandon.

When we're ready, I count off and Brandon starts the piece with the cello. Sebastian comes in on his drum machine after a couple of measures. Sebastian's beats are simple at first and a little thin, but he's setting the tempo. Lily begins twisting and turning, contorting her body to the music. I take out my bow and begin playing long sustained notes, holding them longer than Brandon's, so as I finish one, he's already on to the next. It's like a call and response.

As the beats become more intricate, Lily uses them as markers, making her movements more angled, sharp. She pops and juts her body to the rhythm.

I switch to pizzicato, plucking the bass lines. We play for a couple of minutes before I give the signal to stop.

Pete claps. "That was great, Santos. Really great."

"It was crap," I say.

Lily stands with her hands on her hips. A little sweat forms on her temple.

I add, "Not you, Lily, what you're doing is awesome."

She smiles. "I'm just freestyling." Her smile is the kind that makes you want to lean in closer.

"No, no, it's going to be good," Sebastian says. "It's rough, sure, but once you write what we'll actually be playing . . . I can hear it."

"We'll be playing when the models walk the runway, right?" Brandon asks.

"Yes and no. Okay, here's the show. I wrote it all down." Pete opens his sketchbook and explains his concept, which is big and extravagant and completely Pete, but I have no idea if we'll be able to pull off.

"Cool," Lily says when he's done. "So how many dancers are you thinking?"

"Seven? Can you get me that many?"

"Done."

"So I have to be a model now?" Brandon asks, looking worried. "I'm not going shirtless."

"Neither am I," Sebastian adds.

I shake my head no when Pete looks at me.

"Cowards," Pete says. "I'll need to take all your measurements. Lily, we'll have to talk costumes for the dancers, too."

"Sure. Are we done, then?" Lily says.

I check the time. "We have ten minutes or so. Let's keep playing, see what we come up with. Can you dance again?" I ask Lily.

"Yeah."

Lily interprets the music so effortlessly that I find myself inspired. Next to Levon, she's probably the best dancer I've seen at the school. She'd be the perfect muse, not just for this show, but for my senior recital at the end of the year. Pete asks me something as I'm playing; I nod my head. My focus is on Lily. Her movements are the beginning of a feeling that's contagious and grows with each measure. It takes me a beat before I recognize it: hope.

I didn't realize I'd agreed to go to the fashion district with Pete after school, but I guess I did. He told Sebastian he'd be my ride home, too. Pete also ropes in Lily because he wants to go over fabric for the dancers' costumes.

"How long is this going to take?" I ask Pete as he parks in a tagged-up lot surrounded by a chain-link fence.

"Not too long. An hour?"

I've only been down here one other time, which was also

with Pete when he recruited me for a different project. The
fashion district is located in downtown LA, and it reminds me
a little of being in certain parts of Mexico. Each store has reams
and reams of multicolored fabric in their front windows and
spilling out onto the sidewalk. Since we're here in the afternoon,
it's crowded and the streets have that too-many-people smell of
BO and milk, which makes me want to gag.

Pete takes us to his usual haunts. In one of the larger stores,
I have to pause so I don't get dizzy. The walls have rolls of fabric piled to the ceiling. There're too many bright colors in one
place. Pete and Lily walk through the aisles as if they know
exactly what they're looking for. He stops in front of a ream of
a camouflage.

"Yes. For the bottoms, for sure," Lily says.

"You planning an eighties retro look?" I ask as I touch a
black piece of velvet from a nearby ream.

Pete glances at Lily as if to say, *See what I put up with?*

"In due time, my friend," he says. "In due time. Maybe this
can be for you."

"For me?" I ask.

"Yeah, remember, you're part of the show." He holds the
camouflage up to my face as if he's testing the color.

"Pete, nothing embarrassing, okay?"

"It'll be my designs. When have they ever been embarrassing?"

"There was that one—"

"Stop! Freshman year shall not be mentioned."

Pete and Lily continue walking around the store, pulling more fabric and other items on his list, while I find a seat by the door. There are a couple of fashion students here, probably from one of the local colleges. It's easy to tell them apart from the general public who're just trying to get a deal. The students all have that skinny, a little androgynous, funky with their clothes or hair look, like Pete. Pete will be one of them soon. He's hoping to go to Otis, a really good arts school in the area, next year. He's so driven that my lack of plans seems to freak him out a bit, but he doesn't ride me about it.

We leave the store and load up Pete's car.

"That was fun," I say, the sarcasm lost on both of them.

"Yeah, thanks for taking me. I've never been here," Lily says.

"Oh, we're not done yet."

"Lead on," she says.

I groan, but follow the two of them through the tight streets past smaller stores that all look like variations of each other. How many fabric stores could there be? The store clerks perch outside on metallic stools ready to offer you a great deal as soon as you are in earshot. Pete stops at one to buy some lace. Lily waits with me. We lean against a concrete wall.

"I thought you'd be more into fashion," she says.

I think it's supposed to be a compliment. "I like the finished product."

She nods. "Pete's very talented. How long have you known him?"

"Since freshman year. Where'd you transfer from?"

"This terrible school. I moved from Chicago two years ago and my grandma didn't really know about the schools in her area."

"Chicago? That's kind of far."

"Yeah, well, after my mom died, Dad and my sister and I moved in with Grandma. LA's not that bad. The people are cool."

She pulls out her phone and starts texting or whatever.

"I'm sorry," I say, and cringe because I'm saying the very words I hate to hear.

She keeps typing. "It's not your fault she died, but thank you."

I notice her fingers are long and slender. Everything about her is petite, but she's got incredible strength. There was a part in her free styling when she switched to B-boying and performed a one-handed freeze for more than a couple of seconds, then threaded into another handstand.

Maybe it's because of her transparency or because she doesn't really know me, but I say, "My twin sister died last year."

She looks at me. "What was her name?"

"Grace."

"That's pretty. My mom's name was Susan, but everyone

called her Suzie. She had the best laugh. I have an old voice mail of her telling me about this perv that tried to pick her up at a grocery store and she bursts out laughing. I sometimes play it when I miss her. Want to hear it?"

I'm taken aback with how open she is, so I just nod. Lily finds the recording on her phone. She puts the phone on speaker so we can both listen. Her mom tells the story and at the end comes the laugh, deep and rich and explosive. She ends with, "Love you, baby."

I agree with Lily about the laugh.

"What do you miss about Grace today?" she asks, which takes me a little off guard. In fact, the whole conversation is a little unnerving.

"Today?"

"Yeah, like today I miss Mom's laugh, other days it's the way she'd make French toast, a little burnt and crispy."

"I don't know. I . . . How can you just talk about it, about your mom?"

"What's the alternative? Not talking? Then it'd be like she was never here."

She starts typing again on her phone.

Lily shocks me. I mean, could she be more blunt? She's not waiting for me to answer, either. She acts as if she doesn't care if I respond or not. So I decide to offer up: "I guess today it's the fights we'd have in the morning over the bathroom." Grace took forever, so I usually tried to get in there before her, since we shared a shower. But sometimes I didn't make it. I'd pound on the door and tell her it wasn't her personal sauna.

Lily puts her phone in her back pocket. "That's a good thing to miss because it's real. The details are important. They start to fade if you don't work to remember them."

Pete exits and I'm a little disappointed because I was starting to get into our conversation.

"Done?" Lily asks him.

"Almost. Come on."

Pete walks slowly, leading us down one of the alleys, where the feel is more like a foreign bazaar. Tiny stores are all smashed together, selling not just fabric, but clothes, shoes, children's toys, jewelry, clubbing attire, watches, towels, and sports paraphernalia. Everything's cheaply made. You'll save money buying the stuff, but get ready for it to fall apart in a month.

Lily stops at a jewelry case. She picks up a beaded necklace and holds it up to me.

"I'm not a necklace kind of guy," I say.

"Yeah," Pete says, "the only accessories you'll see on Mark are those plugs and beanie."

The way he says "beanie" makes me ask, "What's wrong with my beanie?"

"Nothing."

Lily laughs just like her mom. "Ohh," she says when she sees mannequins wearing leotards and huge multicolored leg warmers in a shop's window. "I'll be back." She enters the store.

"Where'd you find her?" I ask, not daring to trail after her.

"Levon's suggestion. He's too busy with his own senior show."

"She's . . ."

"Great, I know. I knew you two would get along."

"I was going to say 'forward.'"

Lily comes out of the store and smiles at us, holding up a pair of leggings as if she's just found some major score. "Aren't these amazing?"

"Yes," Pete says. "Perfect."

I want to say that *she's* amazing, but I stop myself. Just because she's pretty and talented, and we bonded over each having a dead relative doesn't mean that we have some deep connection. But there is something about her for sure.

That night I get a text. It's from Hanna.

Run?

Now?

Duh.

It's dark out already.

Not a problem. Outside in five.

I open my front door and Hanna is on the sidewalk, bending down over her left leg, stretching. She looks up at me and I burst out laughing. She's wearing one of those headlamps on top of her head.

"Laugh all you want. It's perfect."

"Where'd you get that?"

"I found it in our camping stuff."

I join her stretching. "Can you even run with it?"

She reaches up and pats the bulb. "I tightened it. If not we can strap it to your big head."

I spy her running shoes. "Did you get new shoes?"

"Yeah, Steve got them for me. He said I needed proper running shoes to train. These are supposedly the best."

"Steve's really working hard, huh?" I say as I pull my arm across my chest.

"It can't be too easy to win me over."

"So he's buying your love?"

She stands up. "I didn't say anything about love. Ready?"

She doesn't wait for an answer and starts jogging up the hill. I jump up and quickly catch her.

"We're supposed to be able"—she takes a breath—"to talk a little back and forth"—another breath—"have a pace where we can still"—breath—"have a"—breath—"conversation."

By the time we reach the top, she's too winded to talk. It takes a couple of paces running on the flat road for her to regulate her breathing.

"How do you know that?" I ask.

"I read it somewhere."

I could easily pass her, but I don't. I stay with her and shorten my stride. The sidewalk is wide enough for the two of us to run together. The trick is not making it look like I'm going too slow. She doesn't like charity. She told me if we're going to train together that I shouldn't hold back. I don't see the point in running with her if we're not together.

It's cold out, so we're both in hoodies and sweats. Our breath rises in small puffs in front of us before we race through it. Her lamp provides enough light, like a little bouncing spotlight. A few stars scatter across the sky above us and a quarter moon hangs as if someone painted it. It's a perfect night.

I tell Hanna about the fashion show I've been roped into, but I leave Lily out. I'm not sure what to make of her. Besides, I just had one conversation with Lily. You can't compare one talk with the thousands I've had with Hanna.

"What's Pete making you wear?" she asks.

"I have no idea."

"I'll be there with bells on."

"No, really, you don't have to."

"And miss your fashion debut? I'm there." Then she asks, "How's Sebastian?"

"Fine, I guess." The night air is fresh and smells a little like damp grass because most of the homes we pass have their sprinklers running.

"You haven't talked?" Her voice rises as if she's concerned.

"I just saw him today."

"What's going on with him?"

"He's good."

"So is he seeing anyone? That girl from last year?"

"Mindy?"

"Yeah."

"That lasted a month."

"Oh. Who broke it off?"

"I don't know."

"You don't know?" She turns her head, beaming the light in my face like I'm under interrogation. "How do you not know?"

"He never said." I point in front of us. "Forward." The light shines ahead.

"And you didn't ask?"

"No."

We need to cross the street. Making sure a car isn't coming in the dark, I take her elbow with my hand and guide her across.

"Thanks," she says.

"Yep."

Even though we're now sloping downhill, she actually slows instead of speeding up.

"I don't understand you. If it were my friend, I would've found out everything."

"What's to know? They broke up. He's fine." At least I think he's fine. He's never spoken about her, but I've never asked. Maybe I should check in.

"But maybe he needed to talk it through."

"We did."

"How'd you even find out they broke up?"

It takes me a minute to remember back. "It was right before band practice. He told Charlie and me that Mindy wouldn't be coming around anymore. We said okay, then started playing."

"Oh my gosh!" She throws her arms up in the air. "I'll never understand guys."

"What?"

She laughs.

"Next time, I'll make sure to send him to you."

"Please do."

I think about bringing up River from the other day, like why she was hanging out with him for the second time. But she hasn't mentioned him, so I avoid the subject.

Instead I ask, "How's school going?" knowing she'll carry

the conversation. That's the trick with most girls. If you're ready with a steady flow of questions, she'll keep it going. Grace actually gave me that tip. She said most girls liked to talk, even the shy ones. They love it when the guy asks questions because it shows he is really interested. Honestly, asking questions is a whole lot easier than actually having to come up with what to say. It works every time.

I spend the rest of our run navigating us over and around the tree roots that have broken through the sidewalk. A few times, I have to reach out and steady Hanna. She continues talking, her voice adding to the rhythm of our feet on the pavement.

"Ready for the final stretch?" Hanna asks at the base of our street.

"That a challenge?"

She takes off. "Maybe."

I catch her and blow past, not stopping until I reach her house. Turning around, I see she's only halfway up.

"Brat," she says when she reaches me, and leans forward, her hands on her knees.

"You told me not to hold back."

"Yeah, but—"

"Oh, so you wanted me to throw it."

"No, just not annihilate me."

Hanna straightens up, takes off the headlamp, and smoothes

down stray pieces of hair. "Ugh. I'm a mess. Time for a shower."

From where I'm standing, she's anything but a mess. In the subtle light, I can see that her cheeks and nose are red. Her eyes are shining. Her black leggings cling to her, showing off her legs. She smiles up at me, looking for me to agree with her.

"You're beautiful," I say, and I'm suddenly shy, so I look at the ground. "But you already know that."

"Thanks," she says.

I look back at her, and this time she avoids my eyes. "It's just a compliment. Don't let it go to your head."

She pushes me. "No take-backs."

I hold up both of my hands. "No take-backs."

It was a rule the three of us had. When you said something nice about someone, you couldn't take it back. It was also true when we said something mean.

"Good job." She holds up her hand for a high five. I give her one.

"See you later," she says, and turns to go to her house.

"Later."

I jog across the street, feeling tired and energetic at the same time. I don't know what made me tell her, but I don't regret it. It's true. Hanna's always been beautiful, especially because she doesn't even realize it.

• • • •

After I shower and am ready for bed, I take out Grace's journal. Lily's comment earlier about remembering the details has me wanting to spend time with Grace. I open it and reread the part where she says she doesn't want to be a twin. This time I'm not so angry. If I'm honest with myself, I've thought the same thing. I remember when we were kids I went through this phase when I wanted a brother instead of a sister. I started calling her George. She retaliated by calling me Marcie. We used the names later to tease each other.

I turn to a different page, and as I read, I can hear Grace's voice in my head.

I have so many fears. I'm afraid of failing, of looking bad, of disappointing people. I'm afraid of risk. I'm afraid of spiders and praying mantises. I'm afraid of public speaking. I'm afraid of losing people I care about. I'm afraid that I won't be remembered, that when I die, I'll be a small exhale, a tiny ripple. I'm afraid of heights and tight spaces. I'm afraid of driving on the freeway in traffic. I'm afraid of really tall people. I'm afraid of tiny dogs and scary movies and being home alone. I'm

afraid of being afraid. It's paralyzing, all
of these fears. Sometimes I sit in the dark of
my room and count to fifty because I think
I see something in the shadows. I'm tired
of being afraid. I want to be more like Mark
or Dad or Jenny. They are never afraid. I'm
the freak of the family. The scaredy-cat. The
one who doesn't belong.

I look up from the page, sad to think that she dealt with so
much fear. We used to count together when we were scared as
kids. I am not as brave as she thought. I'm still not really ready
to know Grace's unfiltered thoughts. What if she becomes more
lost to me? Her journals complicate things because they reveal
parts of her that she withheld from me, from all of us. These
are the parts of Grace that she kept silent and safe. I wonder if
Hanna and I, or my parents, are violating that space by reading
them. I know they've read some of the journals in her room too.

Even this Top Five list of hers. How serious was she about
it? Did she really think she'd accomplish them? She had a million Top Five lists. And here we are implementing one as if it
was her dying wish. But I can't back out. The list has special
meaning now, even if I don't want it to, and not just because
Hanna and I are doing it together.

During one session, Chris said I should practice following through on my commitments. I think he meant school or with my parents. But it just as easily applies to the list. I need to see it through. Maybe I'll find some kind of closure.

I read another page.

Mostly, Hanna is the best friend, but sometimes she's the worst. We're superclose, almost like sisters, and maybe that's the problem. There are times it's as if we're in some competition I didn't know about. Like today, she was totally flirting with River when she knows I like him. It really hurt my feelings. Does she have to have every guy falling all over her?

I close the book and stuff it inside the drawer. I put my headphones in and try to sleep, but the image of Hanna and River in her backyard comes to mind and will not let me rest.

Sixteen

I wasn't planning on telling Dad and Jenny about Grace's list, but the bungee jumping requires two things: parental consent and money. It's more expensive than I currently have the funding for. I bring it up over dinner a couple days before the jump, figuring the less time they have to mull it over, the better.

I clear my throat. "So, I found a journal of Grace's that had a list of five things she wanted to do this year. Hanna came up with this idea to honor Grace by completing her list. That's why we went surfing. Next up is bungee jumping. There's a place just north of here, where Sebastian's cousin went, so it's totally safe and everything. We're going to go on Saturday before it gets too cold. Well, it's never really crazy cold here, but it could be. It's in the mountains." I pull out the form I had printed off the bungee jumping site and hand it to Dad for his signature. "And I need to borrow some cash. I can pay you back. It's sixty-five bucks. Can you pass the chicken?"

I feel both of their eyes on me as Jenny passes the meat. It's probably the most I've said at dinner, at any time actually, in months. Dad reads through the form and hands it to Jenny so she can give it a glance over.

"Bungee jumping? Why would she have wanted to do that?" he asks, his voice softer than usual.

I shrug, willing myself to relax. "The list is like that. Full of surprises." I tell them what else is on it.

"A 5K. That's why you and Hanna have been running?" Jenny asks.

"Yep."

"Can I see the journal?" Dad asks.

"It's in my room." I stand up to get it.

"That's okay, after dinner," he says, flustered. He reads the form again.

"Bungee jumping. That's exciting," Jenny says.

"Maybe I should go with you," Dad says. "It's from a bridge? I don't want you doing anything that could . . ." He stops and Jenny places her hand on his. "How dangerous is it?"

"Zero danger. It's not even that high. Not like jumping in Costa Rica or Africa or something."

Jenny nods her head. "There was that girl who jumped a couple of years ago over those famous falls, what's their name, Victoria Falls? In Zambia? The rope broke and she landed in the river with alligators." Jenny stops when she sees the look I'm giving her. "She lived of course. Besides, that's another country, and the safety precautions in the States are much better. It's fine, honey. Want some more rice?"

"No, thank you. Is there a river under the bridge?" Dad asks.

"Yes," I say, but I have no idea if there's actually water in it this time of year.

"Can I come?" Fern asks.

"Not this time, sweet pea," Jenny says.

"But I want to do Grace's things."

"They're all grown-up things," Jenny says, "but maybe we can come up with something special to do for Grace."

"Okay. I want to see an alligator. If you see one, Mark, take a picture." Fern tells us about the difference between alligators and crocodiles and how someday she wants to be a zookeeper, but only if she doesn't have to clean up the poop. I get that; no one wants that job.

Dad reluctantly signed the release form after reading every word on the website and with Jenny's encouragement gives me the cash, so I head out to Heaton Flats Campground with Sebastian and Grace on Saturday morning. We meet our instructors, two white outdoorsy guys named Whitney and Rick, at the Forest Service Gate.

We're not the only people bungee jumping today. There are five Korean kids from West LA, three white ladies about Jenny's age, a married Latin couple, and us. The instructors tell us that we need to get moving because it's a five-mile hike to the bridge.

We start together, then splinter off into our smaller groups within the overall group.

We are at the base of the San Gabriel Mountains, and even with the slight elevation, the temperature drops significantly. I'm glad to be moving to warm up. It also means we probably won't run into rattlesnakes or tarantulas or scorpions. They usually come out when it's hot.

The trail winds along a narrow river, keeping us to the right of the water. It leads us into a huge gorge with tall jagged granite walls. They're stunning, with lines of different colors stretching from a deep adobe to a light pink, carved out from floodwaters over the years. The constant rushing of the river makes us have to speak louder than usual. Five miles isn't that long, but this isn't a flat five miles, and some of the trail is on the sandy riverbed, over boulders, and across rocks.

About two miles in, we run across some men camped by a section of the river that collects in a small pool. They are bent over the water with pans and are sifting through the sand.

Whitney says hello to them and tells us after we pass that they are miners. Go figure. I wonder if they actually find any gold or silver or whatever it is they're looking for.

Sebastian, Hanna, and I have a conversation that loops and winds along with the trail.

"Hanna, what's your take on alien life-forms?" Sebastian asks.

"Seriously?" She looks at me sideways.

"He's very serious," I say.

"I don't know."

"You've never thought about it?" he asks, surprised, as if everyone thinks about aliens with the frequency he does.

"Not really."

"Oh."

"But I guess there could be. The universe is pretty big, right?"

"Big?" Sebastian says. "'Big' is an understatement. It contains billions of stars, stretching out across billions of light-years, containing a trillion galaxies. It's not flat. It curves." He shows us with his hands. "And that's only what we can observe. Yep, pretty big." He points to a big branch that's in front of us. "Watch your step."

"Thanks. Well, how big is a galaxy?"

"You sure you want to get him started?" I ask, although I love hearing Sebastian talk about galaxies and stars. It makes everything seem so ridiculously huge but also connected at the same time.

"A galaxy is like a way to organize, a unit of measurement."

"Like math?" Hanna says.

"Our galaxy, the Milky Way, contains between two hundred and four hundred billion stars alone. A galaxy can typically contain about ten million to a trillion stars."

Even though it's daytime, I look up to try to see all these stars he's talking about. All I see is blue.

"Think of it this way: The sun is a star, right?"

"Sure," Hanna says.

"The Earth has about, what? Seven billion people? So take seven billion humans per star. Now think about how many people could occupy the space in just our galaxy. How many humans per star?" He stops and picks up some of the sand from the riverbed. "More than the number of grains of sand that are on the Earth's beaches." He lets the sand run through his fingers. As it falls to the ground I try to imagine each grain representing a human life.

We start walking again.

"Wow," Hanna says.

"Yeah," Sebastian says.

"So why haven't we discovered aliens?" she asks.

"Well, they wouldn't come from our galaxy. Ours is quite small in comparison to others, and if there were space-traveling civilizations, it would seem they would have made contact. But it's still plausible."

"You watched a lot of science fiction as a kid, didn't you?"

"Of course, but that doesn't mean anything. So let me ask you again. What's your view on alien life?"

"The probability seems very high," Hanna says, making me smile. Sebastian has converted her in five minutes. "But I think it's like those miners, except sifting through galaxies and infinite space. Finding other life-forms would take lifetimes, maybe all time." She pauses and looks up at the sky. "But it doesn't mean they aren't out there."

Sebastian stops. He begins clapping. "Bravo." He bows in Hanna's direction. "And my job is done." She gives a small curtsy and laughs.

Hanna doesn't realize it, but she's made Sebastian's day. I'm glad they're getting along. Grace always liked Sebastian too.

"What about the parts we can't observe?" I ask.

"What about them?"

"Could there be other universes? Other realities?"

"Sure." Sebastian practically starts skipping along our trail. His enthusiasm pulls us forward with him. "'Multiverse' is what the theory is called. So if time and the universe are infinite, by the law of probability, we can say that there are an infinite number of worlds and people. Or even parallel universes, universes where our choices actually create side-by-side worlds, where we are different versions of ourselves."

"So you're saying there's another Mark out there who is doing or thinking the same thing that I am at this moment."

"Possibly."

"Like someone's doing this." Hanna jumps up and kicks her legs in the air like a frog.

"Let's hope not," I say.

She sticks her tongue out at me.

"It's more like there being a world where I didn't choose to learn the drums. Maybe I don't play music at all. How would that alter my life? I probably wouldn't know Mark, wouldn't know you, and wouldn't be walking this trail right now."

"But we make choices all the time," I say. "There'd be an infinite number of parallel universes then. Kind of seems impossible."

"I don't know. It'd be like the Internet, always expanding," Hanna says.

If I had turned left that night, maybe Grace would be sitting at home, writing in her journal. Or out with River. Or playing with Fern. Or cooking with Jenny. Or sharing a cup of tea with Dad in the kitchen. I see the infinite possibilities of Grace.

"There really wouldn't be any death, then," I say. "Even if you die in one universe, your other self goes on living."

"That's one way to think about it, but it's not like you'd ever know. If the universes came into contact, they'd implode."

We round a curve and an old arch bridge suddenly rises

above us. I do a double take because the bridge looks like a smaller version of the Colorado Street Bridge. Whitney tells us it was built in the 1930s to connect to a tunnel in the mountain, but it was never finished, so it literally dead-ends into the side of a mountain. It's called the Bridge to Nowhere. It's so odd. There's something science fiction about it, but maybe that's all Sebastian's crazy talk about parallel universes.

At the top of the bridge, there's a white tent set up with the bungee jumping equipment. Whitney walks us through a demonstration, how he'll put on the harness, and the three different ways we can jump. There's the swan dive, basically hurling yourself off the bridge face-first. There's the backward leap, where you jump back without looking. The third option is the elevator fall, where you fold your arms across your chest, jump back a little off the bridge, and fall straight down, feetfirst.

Beneath the bridge the river tumbles over huge boulders, which look as if they've been piled to dam the flow, but the water finds a way over and around them. This river would clearly not break your fall, more like break your body, if you dropped into it.

Hanna is very quiet as she eats a granola bar. I pull out my phone and record her.

"How are you feeling?" I ask, thinking maybe the hike has been a little much for her.

"Terrified." She peers down at the river, so I'm capturing only her profile.

"You're not backing out, are you?"

"No." She faces the phone, resolved. "It's not about me." She gives a scared smile, which makes me want to hug her.

What's it about? I think. *Grace?* She's not even here. She's split across universes, a fragment of the Grace I know. Or she's a soul without a body. I like to think she's in a space called Heaven. A place with no more suffering. No more pain. But without those things, is she even human anymore? Because how can you really know joy if you don't know despair? Nothing exists without its opposite.

Does Grace miss me? Does she remember me?

One of the older women volunteers to go first. She makes the rest of us look like chickens because we all avoided Whitney's eyes when he asked who's ready to jump. Rick straps her in, puts a helmet on her head, and helps her climb over the side of the railing.

"Go, Mary!" her friend yells.

She gives a thumbs-up and Rick starts the countdown. We all join him.

"Five, four, three, two, one."

She opts for the swan dive. Mary jumps forward. She stretches her arms out. Her body does a flip right before the rope snaps her back up and she flies toward us before falling again.

Even above the roar of the water, I can hear her laughing.

"If she can do it, I can," Hanna says. "I wish Grace were here." Her eyes water, so she turns away from Sebastian and me.

"How would she have done it?" Sebastian asks.

"Jumped?" she asks.

"Yeah, the elevator?" Sebastian asks.

"No," Hanna and I both say.

"The swan?" Hanna asks.

"The swan," I agree.

Grace didn't like heights, but she didn't like not seeing what was coming even more. We went rock climbing last year with River and his dad up in Joshua Tree. Grace got scared about halfway up. She clung onto the side of the rock. River tried to talk her down, but she wouldn't listen to him. I was right above her and had to get her to visualize where to put her feet. Once she saw the route, she gained her confidence and gradually didn't need me anymore.

Grace didn't like surprises. She liked to know where she was going. When she was really little, she used to have a thing for maps. Memorizing routes, planning the best way to get around Los Angeles. When we'd go on vacations, my dad would refer to her for directions.

There was only one direction she could go when she bungee jumped off the bridge, and that was down, but she'd want to have the full view.

Hanna wants to get it over with, so she's next. She looks cute in the helmet. It kind of reminds me of when she and I used to skate as kids. She keeps her eyes on mine as Whitney tightens the gear. I take her hand and tell her she'll do great. Whitney and I help her over the rail. She doesn't let go of my hand.

"Ahh," she says. "I don't know. I don't know."

"You'll do great. Don't think about it," Whitney says.

"Mark?"

"You can do it," I say. "For Grace." I pry her hand free of mine.

"Okay. Okay. For Grace."

"Five. Four. Three. Two. One!"

Hanna jumps and screams the whole way down. I watch her bob a couple of times until she's pulled back up.

When she's back on the bridge again, her face is flushed and she's grinning.

"Wow. That was amazing." She hugs me so tight that I feel her heart racing.

"Want to go again?" I ask.

"Never! Sebastian, you're up."

Sebastian decides to go backward. He doesn't want to see. He closes his eyes and hops off. But he gets twisted around and he ends up falling face-first. He doesn't make a sound, but I know he's terrified. He's a little shaky when they pull him over the railing. He gives me a weak smile.

Whitney doesn't need to help me over the rail. This rail is shorter and much easier to climb than the one on my bridge. There are no suicide bars here. It's kind of ironic: Here on the Bridge to Nowhere, people pay money to perform a mock suicide. Perfecting their jump, wanting the rush of knowing a small cord is the only thread keeping them from their death.

"Ready?" Whitney asks.

I nod.

"For Grace," I whisper.

"Five. Four. Three. Two. One!" everyone hollers behind me.

I hurl myself as far away from the bridge as I can. I imagine I'm jumping through a portal in time and space. It's as if Grace is jumping with me. She reaches out to hold my hand. We're flying, sailing through dimensions, as if each universe is a color in a rainbow. And in each one she is happy. She is alive. She smiles at me, revealing that small space between her two front teeth.

There's a snap and Grace's hand is torn from mine. My body jerks up as I reach out, trying to find it.

"Grace!"

The granite walls surround me and the rush of the river is louder and more present in my ears. I feel her death all over again. Grace is gone, forever. I am still here, trapped in a world without her. I go limp as they pull up my dead weight.

Seventeen

At night I pull out my phone to find a text from Lily. We had exchanged numbers after the last practice. I didn't think she'd actually use mine.

Today I miss when she'd make me tea and we'd talk.

Her words pick at a scab. Just when I think it's healing, the wound keeps breaking open. The bungee jump helped clarify that. I don't respond.

I take out a piece of paper and begin writing at my desk.

Top Five Things to Do When Bored
1) Eat
2) Watch TV

3) PLAY VIDEO GAMES
4) GO FOR A DRIVE
5) PLAY BASS

I'm tempted to go to the bridge again, but it's not as if that'll make me feel better, so I write:

TOP FIVE REASONS NOT TO GO TO THE BRIDGE
1) COLD
2) PATHETIC
3) GRACE ISN'T THERE
4) NEED TO MOVE FORWARD
5) COLD

Apparently I'm not as creative with the list thing as Grace was. There's a noise coming from the hallway, so I go investigate. The light is on in Grace's room. I push open the door. Fern is looking through drawers.

"What're you doing?" I survey the room to make sure she hasn't made a mess. Everything's exactly where it should be, where it's been for months, undisturbed. Someday we'll have to sift through Grace's belongings. Dad and Jenny are waiting on me, but I haven't been ready.

"Looking for something."

"What?" I'm actually curious. What would Fern need in here?

"A pink scarf."

I point to the bottom drawer, the one where Grace kept her accessories. "Did you try that one?"

Fern sighs. "Yes, but it's not there."

"Isn't it past bedtime?"

"Mr. Fox is going to a party and he needs it." She holds up a stuffed animal for me to see.

I open Grace's closet and her smell hits me. Grace's smell. I hold on to the door frame because it almost knocks me over.

"Good idea," Fern says behind me. She pushes past me into the closet, moving aside Grace's shirts and jeans. Grace always ironed and then hung her jeans. They were perfectly organized, as if she were going to come and pull out a pair to wear tomorrow.

"Oh, here it is!" Fern says, and tries to pull the scarf off a hook. I help her get it down and she holds it tight against her chest. "Thank you, Mark!" She runs off into her room.

I close Grace's closet.

I walk around the room, touching things as I go. Her dresser. The corner of her bed. The top of her computer. A book on her shelf. I open a drawer. Inside are Grace's journals. I pull out my phone and text Lily.

Today it's her smell.

Grace's scent lingers like the wet smell after a rain. I wonder how long it'll be before it leaves altogether. I shut the drawer, turn off Grace's light, and exit the room.

My phone rings with an unknown caller, and I answer, expecting Lily's voice.

"Hello?"

"Hi, Mark."

Mom's voice comes across a little too peppy. She's calling from a number I don't recognize. Smart.

"Hey."

"Is this a good time?"

"Yeah, sorry, it's been crazy busy. New school year and all." I lie, but I know she doesn't want to hear the truth. The truth is I don't want to talk with her.

"How's school going?"

I force myself to answer. "Good."

"And your music?"

"Good." I stand in front of my window facing the street. Hanna's light is on.

"I'm glad. It would be nice to meet up soon. Maybe you can come down to the house for dinner?"

I don't answer right away. The drive to her house would be at least an hour. I don't want to go that far.

As if she can sense my debate, she says, "I could come up and take you out if that's easier. There's a really good sushi place downtown I've been wanting to try."

Downtown. That'd be meeting her halfway. I lie on my bed, not wanting to deal with planning a dinner with Mom. I can't avoid her forever, though. "Yeah, sushi's good."

"How's next Friday night?"

Friday is so soon. I also might have a rehearsal, but I don't check my calendar. "Um, I have something going on."

There's a pause on her end. "Why don't you think about it and call or text me a date."

"Okay."

"Mark, I . . ." Her voice cracks, and I suppose it should make me feel something, but I don't allow it.

"I'll let you know," I say, closing my eyes and squeezing my temple with my free hand.

"Thanks, Mark. I'll see you soon."

"Bye." I hang up the call. She sounds down, but I can't help her. I'm not strong enough to carry her through this. I can barely lift myself.

When Mom left, she didn't even say good-bye. She just took off and didn't see us for a long time—months. Grace used to cry about it. I had to be strong for her. I'd hold her and try to comfort her. What Grace didn't know was that I cried too. It was a silent kind of cry, into my pillow, so no one would hear me. When it was clear Mom wasn't coming back, I made a vow that I wouldn't cry over Mom again. And I've kept it ever since.

In fact, I never cry. Not about Mom. Not about Grace. Not about anything. Chris said I'm emotionally detached. I experience emotions, I'm just selective about showing them. I don't see how tears will help me. They don't change anything. They can't bring someone back. If they could, Mom would have picked up the phone years ago.

I grab my electric bass and begin messing around. I play until I'm in that space where I have no concept of how long it's been, but it doesn't matter. I keep playing and playing, safe inside the music.

Eighteen

Hanna invites Sebastian and me to a football game. I'm a little wary of it. The last time I was at her school was for a track meet with Grace. We had watched River win pretty much all of his races, which I admit was fun. I'm worried now I'll just be reminded of Grace. But Sebastian really wants to go, probably because this is a novelty for us. We attend an arts high school, so we don't have a football team or any other sports team. We don't have a mascot. We don't have pep rallies. We have art. And artists don't usually charge each other in the middle of a field, trying to rip each other's arms off.

I like football, but I don't get as into it as the guys who memorize stats and follow teams. I watch it when it's on, but I'm not a fanatic. What I really love is ice hockey. When it's hockey season, you can usually find my whole family in front of the TV, especially if it's the Kings. Dad tries to get tickets to at least one home game.

When Sebastian finally parks, what seems like miles from the stadium, Hanna asks us, "You guys ready for this?"

"What's this sport called again?" Sebastian says in a sportscaster voice. "Where young men risk their lives in the arena? Where they engage in an epic battle of courage and warfare?"

"You're kind of snarky," she says.

"Snarky? That's a new one." He takes it as a compliment.

Hanna already has our tickets, so we bypass the line at the booth and enter the stadium. At the top of the bleachers, I survey the field. The floodlights illuminate the turf, like it's a huge stage. The air is crisp and charged with anticipation. Old-school AC/DC is blaring. People of all ages are in attendance, not just students. A blond girl calls and waves to Hanna from lower in the stands.

We follow Hanna down the stairs. As we do, a man's voice booms over the speakers, inviting us to welcome the opposing team to the field. Yells come from the opposite side of the stadium, where their players burst through a large paper sign that their cheerleaders hold. They run single file and form a circle, beginning their warm-up by doing jumping jacks.

"Hey, Stacy!" Hanna says to the girl.

"Hey! We saved you seats. Scoot," she says to a couple of people.

They shift over and we file in. Sebastian and I are split up.

I'm next to Hanna and on the other side of her is this black guy she introduces as Tyson. The bleachers are a gray, cold metal that I can feel through my jeans. I pull my beanie down, wrap my black scarf tighter around my neck, and stuff my hands in my jacket pockets. It's going to get cold.

"Everyone, this is Mark and Sebastian," Hanna says.

We give the obligatory male head nods. Tyson, Stacy, Rachelle, Jamal, Freda, and Vince. Their names stick in my memory like tacks on a corkboard. I think I recognize the girls, but I can't place why. Maybe they knew Grace.

The announcer calls out the home team and everyone jumps to their feet like a single organism. A male cheerleader comes out doing a series of flips, which makes the crowd cheer even louder. The team runs onto the field after him and circles up like their opponents, but their warm-up is a little more exciting. They run in place, then drop to the ground and do push-ups, then jump back up.

When we sit back down, Hanna is beaming at me. "Fun, right?"

I nod. "Think the Eagles will win?"

"I don't know. I hope so."

"They'd better," Tyson says. I peg him immediately as one of those guys who overly cares about stats and draft picks.

The players are done warming up, so they take their positions on the sidelines. The cheerleaders perform a cheer for us, which most of the crowd seems willing to follow. Cheerleaders. This is something our school needs. Girls in short skirts and tight shirts, jumping up and down and kicking their legs in the air. I could get used to that. They could encourage us right before recitals or productions. Yeah, they could cheer in between performances. Instead of "Be aggressive," they could chant, "More vibrato," or "Stay on pitch." It would be pretty good motivation, I tell you, especially if they looked like the girl down there with the short black hair. She's all legs.

The teams take the field. We're not superclose, but I can see their breaths coming out in short spurts, as if they're horses being held at the line before battle. The whistle sounds and the Eagles have the ball. The first play is a running one that gets them a couple of yards. I'm not invested in either team, but I hope it's going to be a good game.

Hanna and her friends chat around me, laughing, sharing jokes and an intimacy that comes from attending the same school. Sebastian has no problem engaging. He fits right in, talking to Freda and Jamal about the galaxies. I imagine that I've been plucked from one of his parallel worlds. In my world, Grace would be sitting here at the game with all of her friends, laughing, and talking about stupid things. As if I'm part of some cruel joke, I've replaced her. It feels wrong. Hanna keeps trying to get me to engage in small talk. She can't see that I'm struggling, or if she does, her way of helping isn't working. I want to be left alone.

"Tyson just moved this year," Hanna offers.

"Oh yeah? From where?" I ask, trying to be polite.

"Boston."

He sits hunched forward. His eyes never leave the field, as if he's completely mesmerized with the game. He's a big guy, probably an athlete too.

"You play?" I ask.

"I used to, but I had to pick between football and basketball. I chose basketball."

"What position?"

"Center."

"Tyson's starting this winter," Hanna says.

"Too bad you don't like basketball," I say.

"You don't like basketball?" Tyson seems disappointed.

"Well, it's not that I don't *like* it," she says, shooting me a look. "I haven't really watched it much."

"Really? I've heard you say watching basketball is as boring as waiting for paint to dry." I'm picking a fight, and I don't even know why.

"Mark, you're funny." She laughs nervously.

"Hopefully you'll come to my games," Tyson says, smiling at her before going back to watching the field. I don't like what he's implying, but it's stupid because why the hell should I care about the way he looks at her? I let my eyes linger on the cheer-leader down in front.

"You should come too," he says to me.

"Maybe," I say.

Leaning into me from behind, her knees pressing into my back, Stacy says, "Mark, how are you doing?" She says the words as if we are close friends.

"Great, you?"

She bends near my ear. "Grace was a friend of mine." She squeezes my shoulder. "We had English last year. She was such a good writer. I didn't get to tell you at the funeral, but I wanted you to know she is very missed."

That's why she looks familiar. There was a whole contingent of Grace's school friends at the funeral. Some guys dressed in barely worn black suits and girls walking awkwardly in heels as if they were playing dress-up. I avoided them. I take a deep breath and hold it, counting before I release it slowly.

"You okay?" Hanna asks me and puts her hand on my thigh. Maybe in any other situation I would love for Hanna to be touching me, but right now it chafes.

"Perfect." I remove her hand.

One of the Eagles players receives a red card. "Boo!" the fans cry out.

"How was bungee jumping?" Tyson asks Hanna.

"Crazy! I was so scared, but once I got over the fear of the actual jump it was fun. The hike in was the hardest."

"What's next on the list?" Stacy asks.

"Spoken word, I think. Right, Mark?"

Suddenly I'm in a nightmare. Discussing Grace and her Top Five with total strangers? I can't believe Hanna told them.

"Who's going to do it?" Tyson asks.

"Me," Hanna says.

"I want to come," Tyson says.

"Sure, I'll let you know the plans."

"I think it's awesome what you guys are doing," Stacy says. "Grace would have loved it."

"I'm sorry about Grace," Tyson says to me. "I didn't know her, but from what I've heard, she was an amazing person. I can't imagine what it'd be like to lose a sister."

"No, you *can't* imagine." I churn out the words like I've got dirt in my mouth. Inside I'm seething. I try to turn the switch off, set it to neutral, but it's too late. I don't give him the chance to say anything else. "I'd rather not talk about it."

He turns his attention back to the game. Now there's something more than excitement in the air between us.

Hanna does that nervous chatter thing, but I'm not listening anymore. I'm sitting there, but I'm not here. I'm not really anywhere. I stare at the field.

Hours or minutes later, Sebastian taps me on the shoulder. "It's halftime. Want to get something to eat?"

Hanna has her back to me and is listening to something Tyson's saying.

"You okay?" Sebastian asks.

"I'm fine. Actually, I've got to go. You ready?" I don't wait for Sebastian to answer. I get up and cross over Hanna and Tyson. "Hanna, you can get a ride with Tyson or someone, right?"

"You're leaving?" she asks, surprised.

"Yeah, I've got to do something."

I don't bother waiting for her reply. I climb the steps, anxious to get away from all the people and the noise.

Outside of the stadium, I hear Hanna calling my name.

"Mark!"

I don't turn around; instead I keep walking toward the car.

"Mark! Where are you going?"

I stop, confused for a moment about where I am. The cars blur and my head feels fuzzy. "I'm sorry, but I forgot I have to practice. It's a good game. Really. Thank you for the invitation."

"What's wrong?" She says the words like *I'm* the one who's ruining *her* night.

"Nothing. I've just got something to do."

I head down a row, but I can't find the car. *No, it must be the next row.* I turn around.

"Can you wait?" she asks. "You're not making sense." Her voice is shaky, and I can't tell if she's angry or going to cry. Sebastian is next to her.

"Why'd you tell them about Grace's Top Five?" I say louder than I intend, practically yelling at her.

"I didn't think it was a secret," she responds.

"You act like we're running around earning Brownie patches for doing good deeds." I pace in front of them.

"That's not true. We never said we couldn't tell other people."

"It's private. You shouldn't just go blabbing about it to anyone. You should have asked me first."

"I'm sorry." She holds out her hands like a peace offering. "I didn't know it would upset you. They're my friends. They were *Grace's* friends."

I grunt. "They barely even knew her."

"What are you talking about? Of course they knew her! They saw her every day at school. She had a life, you know: a boyfriend, friends, teachers."

I get real close so that she stumbles back. "Oh yeah, River. I've noticed how you've jumped right in there."

"What's that supposed to mean?"

"Hanna," Sebastian interjects. "Maybe I should talk to Mark."

She holds up her hand to stop him. "I can handle Mark. What're you saying?"

"Now that Grace's gone, there's an opening and you've taken it. I get it. He's Mr. Sensitive, pouring out his feelings. Great boyfriend material."

"I hate when you do this." Her eyes well up with tears.

Seeing her tears gets me going, and I can't help it. I spit out the words, knowing I'm hurting her. "When I do what, Hanna? When I want to go home because I don't think going to a crappy high school football game and watching you flirt with every guy here is the best time of my life?"

She wipes her eyes with the sleeve of her jacket and says softly, "When you push away the people who care about you and act like an asshole."

"Asshole. Wow. Remember, there are no take-backs, Hanna, not just for the good things."

"Knock it off," Sebastian finally says.

Hanna is openly crying now. Sebastian puts his arm around her, and that just sets me off again. When did he choose her side? "Are you seriously going to cry? You're always crying, Hanna. What do you have to cry about? What a joke."

"I said, knock it off."

I glare at Sebastian. "I don't have time for this. Let's go."

He looks at Hanna. "I'm staying."

"Fine. Give me your keys." I hold out my hand.

"No," he says.

I get in his face. Sebastian doesn't back down. His expression is fixed like his stance.

"I don't need your shit either, Sebastian." I push him and am surprised at how solid he is. He doesn't even move. I push him again, this time hard enough to make him stumble back a few steps.

"Mark!" Hanna steps in between us. Her hand presses against my chest. "Why don't you just come back to the game? Let's sit down. Talk it through."

I step back. "I don't want to talk." *I don't want to say something mean, to hurt you.* My head is throbbing. "You want me to act like everything's normal because someone scores a touchdown? As if all I need is a good game to make me happy?"

"No," Hanna says. "I know everything's not fine. I know you're still hurting."

"I don't feel anything. Right now, I don't care." I point at her. "I don't care about you." I point at Sebastian. "Or him or anything." I throw my arms out to include the whole world. "I just need to go home."

Two girls approach us. "Hi, Hanna. Everything okay?"

"We're fine," she says.

"Yes, thank you for asking," Sebastian says, and pulls Hanna even closer, comforting her.

One of the girls eyes me, and I give her a large, fake smile.

"Halftime is almost over."

"Thank you," Hanna says.

The girls walk away and the three of us stand there in silence for a few moments. Sebastian's arm is still around Hanna, so I step forward and hit him in the mouth. My hand hurts, like the time I hit River. But Sebastian doesn't just stand there and take it. He lunges for me, knocking me down on the pavement. We roll around, both of us trying to get in punches, until I push him off and scramble to my feet.

I start walking away because I don't have anything to say that I won't regret later. I can walk home. No one calls after me.

But I don't go home. I end up at the bridge.

"Grace?" I whisper. All I hear is the water below and the cars on the nearby freeway.

I stand on a concrete bench and hold out my hands, as if I can touch the seam that will spill me into the universe Grace now inhabits, but all I touch is air.

I think maybe I'm losing it. This is the beginning of crazy. And it's not a good crazy. It's the kind that requires drugs and institutionalization. It's the kind of crazy where I become someone I don't want to be and alienate everyone I know. I lean against the suicide bars.

"I really messed up," I say as if Grace can hear me.

But she can't hear me because she's gone. It's only me now. I don't feel her anywhere. I only feel the cold.

• • • •

When I open the front door of the house, Jenny is in her pj's, sitting on the couch in the living room with a cup of tea.

"How was the game?"

"Sucked." I sit down across from her. I kind of feel like talking to Jenny about my night, but I kind of don't.

"I didn't hear Sebastian pull up."

"I walked home."

She takes a sip of her tea.

"I went to the bridge," I say before she can ask.

"And?"

"And nothing. I just walked around."

"Do you go there a lot?"

I nod. "It's the last place . . . well, it's where Grace . . ." I don't know what else to say. I'm too tired.

Jenny puts her cup on the coffee table. She leans toward me, her hands folded in front of her, resting on her knees. "I'm a light sleeper. Drives your dad crazy. When you first started taking off at night, I was worried, but you always came home. I began checking on you, making sure you were in your bed." She chuckles. "It's like I have a baby all over again. I haven't slept through the night in months."

The fact that Jenny knows that I sneak out of the house and has been checking on me makes something catch in my throat. "Does Dad know?"

She nods and offers me her tea.

I take a sip and cough before placing it back on the table. "Geez, Jenny. What's in this?" I know she likes it strong, but there's thick dregs that I accidentally swallow.

"Good stuff, don't worry. Come here." She pats a spot on the couch.

I get up and sit next to her, like when Grace and I were little. I'd sit on one side, Grace would get on the other side and Jenny would put both arms around us and squeeze us tight. She called us her gift because she thought she couldn't have children. That was before she had Fern, of course. Fern, she called her miracle. But she never made us feel like she loved Fern more.

Now I'm bigger than Jenny, so I pull her into me. She rests her head under the crook of my arm, like she's more of a sister than a stepmom.

"Your dad is worried about you. He doesn't know how to talk to you. I think he's afraid that he's losing you, too."

"Dad and I have never been close," I say.

"Not true. It just feels that way now, so that feeling is coloring everything."

"Maybe."

"You guys need to find your way back, meet each other halfway."

I don't know how to find my way back. I don't even know

what that means. My knuckles are sore, so I rub them a little. They're red and swollen from where they made contact with Sebastian's face.

"Jenny, I think it's time for me to replace the car."

"Did you get in a fight with Sebastian?"

"Kind of."

"I guess that's a good enough reason."

"Can you tell Dad?"

"Yeah. Mark?"

"What?"

"You're my favorite," she whispers.

Jenny was always calling each of us her favorite. When she'd get you a cookie or help you with homework, she'd whisper in your ear, "You're my favorite." I was always her favorite boy. I'd say, "But I'm the only boy." And she'd say, "Exactly."

I don't deserve to be anyone's favorite.

I put my legs up next to hers on the ottoman. We sit that way for a while, until Jenny quietly leaves, tucking a blanket around me, thinking I'm asleep. But I'm wide-awake, replaying the sound of my walking away from Hanna and Sebastian, replaying their silence that followed.

Nineteen

On Sunday night I get a text from Sebastian.

Giving my notice. No longer your personal chauffeur.

I had planned to apologize to Sebastian on Monday morning after we'd each had the weekend to cool off. I figured I'd say I was sorry, he'd say sorry, and that'd be the end of it. The text was a sign that it might not be as easy as I thought.

Then there was Hanna. In less than twenty-four hours it felt like our street had widened. There might as well have been three thousand miles separating us. I wasn't sure how to bridge that gap yet.

Jenny is a little pissed that I lost my ride to school, because now she'll have to drive me. She and Dad come up with a plan. She'll take me and pick me up for a week, and then I'll go car shopping with Dad. If we don't find one, I can take public transportation. Any normal person would be excited about getting a car, but it makes me feel like my hand is being forced. A new car means I'm moving on. I don't know if I'm ready. My response is to put in my earbuds and walk away, which Dad, of course, doesn't take too well. He taps me on the shoulder. I turn around. He motions for me to remove my headphones, so I do.

"I'm not sure what's brought on the attitude, but you're not to treat me or Jenny so disrespectfully. I don't care how you feel, we are not going down that path again. One week." He holds out his hand. When I hesitate, he adds, "Maybe I should make an appointment to see Chris."

With that last threat, I hand him the phone. It's not like I have anyone to talk to anyway.

Before I exit Jenny's car on Monday morning, she tells me to have a good day. Fern wants to hug me again, but I don't. I walk to first period, successfully avoiding any real conversation other than "Hey, what's up?" Sebastian ignores me in English and in theory. I have to give him props on the theory shunning, because I sit right behind him. I stare at the back of his big fat head the whole class, daring him to turn around. He doesn't. At lunch, I head for the roof again. It's empty this time. No Brandon sitting on the air unit. No couples making out.

I stand on the edge facing downtown, as a couple of drops begin to fall. The sky is a dark gray. The heavily blackened clouds droop low, and when I'm thinking it's going to really pour, the sky opens up. I just stand there instead of running for cover. The rain stings my face like tiny wasps, but I welcome the pain. I picture Sebastian's shock after I hit him. Today he's all anger and distance, as if I've crossed a line in our friendship that I didn't even know was there until I was on the other side. I deserve this. I deserve to be alone. I don't need Sebastian. I don't need anyone.

"Santos," Pete calls out, and rollerblades over to me in the hallway. "What the hell happened?"

"What do you mean?" Although it's not a far-out question. I *am* soaking wet.

"With Sebastian. He says you got into a fight."

"Yep." I don't offer an explanation, and try to walk past him. My shoes squish and squeak on the linoleum floor. They're probably ruined.

He rolls next to me. His blades make him tower above me. "It's a couple of weeks until showtime. How long is it going to take for you guys to kiss and make up?"

"I'm not doing it." My voice is dry, detached. With the way Sebastian acted earlier, I know it isn't going to be an easy fix.

"It can't have been that bad."

"The show," I clarify. "I'm not doing the show."

"That's rich."

"You have Sebastian and Brandon. They can get another bassist." I'm shivering now and a little numb.

Pete says, "I was counting on you."

"You shouldn't have."

"You can't quit," he says. "I need you. It's important."

"You don't need me, and I hardly think a stupid fashion show constitutes important." I keep walking, and this time he doesn't try and follow me.

"I thought—" he says behind me, but either I don't hear what he says or he doesn't finish. It doesn't matter. None of it matters.

It's surprisingly easy to go through a whole day at school without talking to anyone. Getting through a whole week, that takes a little bit of strategy. There's my usual tricks: head down, avoiding eyes, looking like I've got places to go and people to see. Since I've ticked off Pete, one of my only other close friends here besides Sebastian, it's not like anyone is trying to engage me. I can do this. I can probably go the whole year without interacting with others. Become a ghost. I've done it before.

Jenny is late picking me up on Friday, so I'm sitting at the designated spot on the curb like a pathetic underclassman when Lily parks herself next to me. *Great.* I get ready to move just in case she tries to talk to me. She doesn't. It may as well be like I'm not even there.

She pulls out a notebook and begins sketching some kind of animal. I watch her for a little while. She's using pencil and smudging lines here and there, focusing on the outline first. The tips of her fingers turn gray.

"So you're an artist too?" I ask, unable to help myself.

"Maybe. What're you doing here?"

"Waiting for my ride."

"Me too."

She adds legs and a head.

"You should do the show," she says.

"Why?"

"Because you're good, and Pete needs you. He's kind of freaking out. It's important not to quit."

"I didn't want to do it in the first place."

"So what? We all do things we don't want to do."

I open my mouth to say something, but nothing comes. Lily doesn't know me. So what if she lost her mom. That doesn't mean that she knows what I've been through. I don't have to listen to her, but I don't really have a comeback, so I watch her draw. When she's finished, she tears the picture from her notebook and gives it to me.

"Here. You're kind of like this now."

I look at the drawing. "A porcupine?"

A car pulls up and honks. Lily gathers her things.

"My grandma says that loving hurting people is like hugging porcupines." She gets up and slings her backpack over her shoulder. "Don't worry. You won't always be a porcupine." With that she walks to the car, opens the door, and gets in.

I stare at the drawing. The porcupine's spikes are sharp and pointy, like they'd make you bleed if you touched them. I think about what I said to Hanna and Sebastian, Pete's face when he realized I really was quitting, the disappointment in my dad's voice . . . I don't want to be this person, but I don't know how not to be him.

That night I stand in front of the entrance to the bowling alley and wait. My stomach feels sick. *I don't really need this. No one is forcing me to go.* A couple steps around me and enters.

What do I have to lose? Everything. "Nothing," I say out loud.

There's a Chinese restaurant just inside the bowling alley and to the left. I wait next to a big gold Buddha sitting by the front desk. A hostess approaches me.

"Table for one?" she asks.

The only people in the restaurant sit at a round table in the back. That has to be the Twinless Twins meeting. "I think I'm with them." I walk through the restaurant, past photos of China hanging on the walls.

"Mark?" A man stands up when I approach.

"Yeah."

He reaches out and shakes my hand. "I'm Greg." He's older than I thought. His dark curly hair is peppered with gray. He's a Latin guy, an inch or two taller than me.

"Hey, guys, this is Mark. It's his first time at a meeting, so let's show him some love." I smile, but inside I'm thinking that I've stepped into some bad movie.

"Hi, Mark," everyone says, and by everyone, I mean a handful of adults my parents' age and older, mostly women. "Um," I say, and look back toward the exit. I've clearly made a mistake coming here.

"Have a seat, Mark." Greg pulls up a chair for me to sit next to him. "Can I get you anything to drink? Eat?"

"A Coke."

These people smile at me and I smile back. I have that same feeling I get when the aunties are going to grill me about my love life, except no one is Filipino.

"We were just getting started. We are going around the table, talking about our twins. Jessica was going to go first."

They get right into things. I sit on my hands because they're suddenly sweaty. Jessica tells about how her twin Lisa died from breast cancer five years ago. Jessica misses their long conversations and traveling together during the summers. After Jessica,

Trudy shares about her twin, Trevor. He died from an overdose of sleeping pills. All of their stories are heavy. Most of them lost their twins years ago. Grace was definitely the youngest twin to pass out of the group.

When it's my turn, I say this: "Grace was killed on the Colorado Street Bridge. I was driving when a car swerved into our lane and hit us head-on. I don't even remember most of it. Just, you know, that she never really woke up. It happened last May, six months ago. She was seventeen." I thought it might be hard to talk about Grace with strangers. But no one here gives me the sad face or looks away awkwardly because they're not sure what to say.

"So recent," a woman says. "It must be very raw."

I shrug and sink a little in my chair, not used to having so many eyes on me. "I can't sleep that well. Sometimes I go to the bridge to try to clear my head." Once I start talking, it's like I have, like, verbal diarrhea or something. I can't stop. "I've even started dreaming about her. Nothing special. I barely remember them. Last night we were eating cereal at the kitchen table."

"I remember after Lisa died, I used to dream about her every night," Jessica says. "At first I was so upset; they were kind of like nightmares. Now they aren't every night and when they come, I try to remember them."

My dreams of Grace felt like nightmares in the beginning too.

"I had this recurring dream where we'd be at a Patriots game.

Same seats. Same game. Same conversation," John says, which I totally get because I've dreamed of Grace and me at a Kings game, or maybe it's more like I'm remembering instead of dreaming.

"Mine used to take me to Disneyland," says Ann, a woman who looks to be in her sixties. "We'd ride our favorite ride, the Pirates of the Caribbean. That drop gets me every time."

It's funny to hear a grown-up so excited about Disneyland. I haven't been since I was a kid.

"The first one you can see coming, but I always forget about the second one." Ann laughs. "I used to hold on to Francie and she'd call me a big baby."

She wipes a tear away from the corner of her eye. "Oh man. For a while, I took nightly trips to Disneyland. Then this one time we were on the ride, heading toward the second drop, and Francie whispered into my ear to let go. So I did, and at the bottom she turned to me and said that she'll always be next to me if I needed her."

Did her twin really talk to her in a dream? Because Grace never speaks to me. Grace hasn't spoken since the night I lost her.

"In the beginning, it's so intense," John says. "Intense grief. Intense loneliness. It's like you're in this cocoon. You have to go through the process of grieving. No one understands the kind of loss you feel because they're not a twin. So they get nervous around you and don't know what to say."

Yeah. And they know you're sad but then they don't want you to be sad anymore. How can you just decide not to be sad anymore?

"Does the loneliness ever go away?" I ask.

"It lessens," Jessica says. "I don't know if it ever goes away. I think that's the twin bond."

"It comes and goes in waves," Ann adds. "What's that saying? Grief is like an ocean? I think it's the same with loneliness. When you're a twin, you have this really unique perspective of identity. You are an individual, sure, but from the beginning, you relate to the world from the position of *we*. So when your twin dies, it's like you have to figure out how to be an *I*, but still honor and carry that *we* with you. Your twin will always be a part of you because she has always been a part of you. I feel like I'm living for the both of us. *I'm* still here, so *we're* still here."

I can't tell if I'm crazy or if everyone is crazy or if we're all a little bit crazy, but these people get me. For the first time since Grace died, I feel understood, without anyone judging or trying to fix my grief.

After everyone's had a chance to share, Greg glances at his watch. "We have a few more minutes. Let's take care of some business items."

They talk about the next meeting, some kind of candle-lighting ceremony over at Griffith Observatory, and a national conference during the summer. This time it's in Los Angeles, so they're all planning to attend.

"Any final questions?" Greg asks.

I raise my hand. "Why a bowling alley?"

Greg smiles. "Because we like to bowl."

"Don't think that Ann here is a pushover," Jessica says. "She looks like a little thing, but she has a mean strike."

Ann smiles shyly.

We take over three lanes, which is fine because it's a weeknight and not a league night, so we pretty much have the place to ourselves. Even though I don't live very far from the alley, I've never bowled before, a confession which gets a lot of exclamations from the group.

"What?" says Trudy. "Okay. We've got the kid. But I'm warning you: Once you start, you'll become addicted."

They're right about Ann. She shuffles up with her ball, which she looks barely strong enough to carry, and in one move, releases it down the lane. It breaks through the pins. They all splinter off with the *crack* of a bat breaking.

Ann saunters back to us. "And that's how it's done."

"Impressive," I say.

I am not so impressive. I've picked a ball whose finger holes are too tight. When I go to release the ball, it sticks before flying out of my hand and getting some nice air, only to *thud* and leisurely roll down the lane. I hit one pin. But my team claps behind me.

"That's all right, Mark."

I try to hide my embarrassment by pulling my beanie low. Ann hands me another ball. "Try this one."

I put my fingers in the holes.

"Better?"

"Better," I say.

Ann stands next to me and talks me through where to stand and what to do. I'm hoping that no one I know comes into the alley. I have no idea how I'll explain bowling with a bunch of old people. But I'm having fun, so I tell myself to get over it. I follow Ann's instructions and release the ball.

"Ladies and gents, Mark's first gutter ball," Greg announces.

They all clap.

"I thought it'd work," I say to Ann.

She shrugs and pats me on the back. "It takes time. You'll get the hang of it."

I don't get the hang of it, but I actually have fun. In the end, my team comes in second. They would have won without me, but Ann just says, "Next time." I nod, surprised that I'm open about coming back to the group.

As we leave, I follow Greg out to his car in the parking lot. He lights up a cigarette. "How was your first Twinless Twins meeting?" he asks.

"Pretty painless," I tell him.

He laughs. "I'm glad you came, Mark. Hopefully we'll see you at the candle-lighting ceremony. Invite your family."

"Yeah. Maybe."

"If you're worried about them not wanting to come, they might surprise you." He tips the ash from the end of his cigarette. "I'd offer you one, but I'd hate to see you begin a dreadful habit. Started after Stephanie died."

"Do you ever get over it? I mean, you guys are laughing, having a good time. Does the guilt ever go away?"

"The world is full of suffering. Sometimes we cause our own suffering, but sometimes we suffer because we're human. We're just standing here and breathing." He takes another drag and lets out the smoke. "It wasn't your fault that Grace died. I don't know why it happened or why you weren't killed instead of her or why you weren't both killed. But you are still here, so that means you have to fight to move forward. You have to choose to live. Because if you don't, then you might as well be dead. And there's no honoring Grace in that."

I lean back against the hood of his car, thinking about what Greg said, thinking about Lily calling me a porcupine too. "I'm so angry," I say. "I think I'll be angry forever."

"I've read these cases about people experiencing such trauma that they think they're paralyzed. There's nothing physically wrong with them, but for some reason, their mind has convinced them that they're paralyzed. And they literally cannot move, though the doctors insist there's no medical reason why they can't."

"Weird."

"Yeah, weird. But here's the thing: The day they decide to walk again, they walk, even run."

"So you're saying that I just need to get up and walk?" I get what Greg's saying, but it sounds impossible. You can't just decide not to miss someone or not to be in pain.

"I'm saying there will come a time when you won't be so angry or in so much pain. It doesn't have to be now. You just have to believe that it'll come and let people in."

"How do I do that? I can't act like everything's fine when Grace is gone."

"No, but for me, I needed to realize I wasn't the only person who'd lost someone."

I think about all the people who lost Grace too: Dad, Jenny, Fern, and Hanna, and even River.

"I also needed to forgive myself."

"For what?" I ask, though I think I know where he's coming from.

"For living."

I let that sink in. "Or I could just take up smoking."

Greg throws his cigarette on the ground and grinds it into the asphalt with his foot.

"Or you could just take up smoking." He laughs. "You game to try a method that helped me?"

"Sure." I shrug, thinking it couldn't hurt.

"Try saying the words 'I forgive myself' at least once a day."

"Seriously? Out loud?"

"I know it sounds weird, but words are magical. Try it." He pats me on the shoulder. "Talk to you soon." He opens the car door and gets in.

I start walking home. Even though there are cars driving by, it's lonesome out. I can't believe I spent the night sucking at bowling. But the people were surprisingly cool. Greg was cool. I wait at the intersection for the light to turn. No one is around me, so I decide to try what he said.

I whisper, "I forgive myself."

Nothing happens. I'm not sure what I'm expecting, but I don't feel any different. Greg said once a day. I should have asked him for how long. It probably doesn't work right away. Nothing of worth happens without effort. It's been months since Grace's death, months where I've lost whole pieces of me, and it might take months to put me back together. I feel stupid talking to myself, but no one is here, so I try it one more time. "I forgive myself." The words are empty and without conviction, but I say them. It's a start. The light turns and I step forward.

Twenty

Dad and I call a truce of sorts, which means I no longer sulk around the house when he's present and he gives me back my phone and takes me car shopping. He actually loves car shopping; he loves the whole game of it. *The salesmen circling us are like bees to honey,* he says. *Bees to honey.* We walk around the lot, looking at all kinds of cars. I have the idea to get an SUV to cart my equipment around. Dad thinks more economically and suggests I go smaller. But my upright will hang outside the window of a small car. I take him over to a slightly used Honda CR-V, the car I had read about online.

"This is the one," I tell Dad.

Dad walks around the car, looking it over. As he's doing so, a salesman in a brown suit approaches.

"Let me do the talking," Dad whispers.

"All yours," I say. I am the opposite of Dad. I hate the whole buying-and-selling dance.

The salesman, Jose, starts a conversation with Dad about teen drivers and Honda's safety rating, and tells us we're lucky to be here today because they just so happened to get this Honda this week. If I don't like the black, they can also find us another in any color we'd like.

Dad tells Jose that we will be paying in cash if we buy a car from him today and asks if we can go for a test drive. Jose quickly leaves to get the keys.

"Well?" I ask Dad.

"Price is too high, but we'll see what you think after driving it. Do you want to try anything else?"

"Yeah." I tell him about the other three cars that I researched on the lot.

"You've done your homework," he says with approval.

"Yep."

"Okay. Let's see if we can get you a good deal."

After two hours, Dad talks the sticker price down six thousand dollars and extends the warranty for one hundred thousand miles, and I drive the CR-V off the lot. It has that new-car smell mixed with a perfumed forest from the green tree hanging from the rearview mirror. I follow Dad in his car over to a sandwich place for lunch.

"How is it?" Dad asks while we are sitting down and waiting for our food.

"Awesome."

"Good. I'm glad you didn't want something flashy. Jenny will like it too. It's a safe, reliable car."

I try something out. "Grace would have liked it," I say.

Dad smiles and tries not to make a big deal about what I've said. He rearranges his utensils on the napkin in front of him. "Yes. She would have."

He gets a phone call and excuses himself, while I sit and play an app on my phone. By the time he's finished, the food has arrived. My roast beef sandwich looks amazing.

"How's practice? Any concerts coming up?" Dad asks, then takes a bite of his ham-and-cheese sandwich.

"Okay. Not for a couple of months." I wipe some mayo from the side of my mouth.

Dad enjoys the concerts we put on at school because he's also a musician. He plays the piano, but now that I think about it, I haven't heard him in a while.

"Dad, how come you don't play the piano anymore?"

"Don't I?"

"No."

"Haven't had the time, I suppose."

Dad takes another bite of his sandwich. Sitting across from him, I notice he looks a lot older. His wide face is more sharp than round. He's got circles under his eyes. There's more gray scattered through his hair. Wrinkles cradle his eyes. People used to say how much Grace and I took after him, and even when I passed him in height, they'd still say it. Dad was never a big man, but I can't remember him being this small and tired.

"So, have you spoken with your mom lately?" he asks, making his voice sound casual.

"We talked." I don't really want to talk about Mom.

"And are you going to see her?" It's a question, not a command.

"Yeah."

"When?"

"I don't know." I stare at my food. "Whenever."

"Look, I've never pushed you where your mom is concerned, but this is different. You need to hear what she has to say. It's not right to keep someone captive."

I don't know what Dad's talking about. Mom is the adult, the responsible party here. "I'm not holding her captive."

"You're not releasing her from her past mistakes. We've all made them. I am far from perfect, but your mom and I worked through our issues long ago. This is something you have to do on your own, and I don't want to force you—"

"Then don't." The words slip out harsher than I intend.

Dad holds up his hands. "Fine." He resumes eating. The silence cuts through any headway we were making by having an actual conversation. We're back to distance and dead ends.

Even though it's not comfortable for me, I make a move. "I know what you're saying, Dad, and I will talk with her. I'm just waiting for the right time."

"Don't wait too long." He puts down his sandwich and holds out his hand for me to shake on it. Dad's had me shaking on deals since I was a kid. He says your word is stronger and more binding than any ink.

I hesitate, but I shake, and he grips my hand tight and searches my eyes, letting go when he sees what he wants to see, I guess.

"I'd like to take Jenny out for dinner and a movie tonight. Can you watch Fern?"

"Yeah." I shrug. "I don't have anything. What movie?"

"Some romantic drama she's been wanting to see. You know, one of those British ones."

"Good luck," I say.

"I know." He shakes his head and chuckles.

I take a drink. Some of the Coke squirts up through the

straw, hitting me in the face and even spraying at Dad. We both crack up.

"Sorry. I don't know how that happened." I wipe the Coke that's dribbling down my face.

"You do have talent." He dabs at his shirt with a napkin. "By the way, how're classes going?"

I know he's asking because last year I bailed on school and barely passed. "Good, more Bs than As."

"That's still strong. What're you studying in English?" Dad loves to talk about books because he has read just about everything.

"At the moment, *Brave New World*, which is way better than *Frankenstein*. Do you know that wasn't even the name of the monster?"

Dad nods. "Of course. It's the doctor's name."

"It wasn't even scary."

"No, it's about what makes us human. It's also about a monster's longing to be loved. Did you know it's considered the first science fiction novel? Pretty ahead of its time."

It feels a little rusty at first, talking with Dad, but pretty soon we're along familiar grooves. Talking books helps. We've always discussed what books I'm reading in English. Even when Dad hasn't read a book, he'll get it and read it just so we can talk.

"Sebastian told me. And did you know it was written by a

girl?" I say. "She made a bet with these guys one rainy night and wrote *Frankenstein*."

"I didn't know that part. Wow. Two SF books this year. I bet Sebastian loves that." Sebastian and Dad have had plenty of discussions about books too—well, mainly SF ones, because that's all Sebastian will read.

"Yeah. I'm only at the beginning of *Brave New World*. It's creepy with all the conditioning and pill popping, but I like creepy."

"It gets even better."

"How's work going?" I ask before he can ask another question.

"Good. The holidays are coming up. I could use you again, if you'd like."

The past two years Grace and I've worked at one of Dad's stores. She braved the shoe department, which was good money, but too cutthroat for me. Your earnings are based on commission, and Grace would tell these crazy stories about how people fought for customers. There was this one guy who actually told Grace she had an important call from Dad so *he* could help one of her customers. The two of them waged a war, where they were civil, but openly battling to see who could sell more shoes in one week. I stayed in the men's section, where we still worked on commission but there was never any drama.

"That sounds good."

"Done."

"Dad?"

"Yes, Mark?

"Thanks for coming with me to get the car."

"You bet." His eyes hold mine, and this time I see not just relief, but something that looks a little like happiness.

Babysitting Fern is basically me putting on one of her favorite shows. I let Fern stay up a half hour later than usual and then send her to bed.

"Good night," I tell her after she's brushed her teeth, I've read her a story, and she is tucked into bed. I turn on her nightlight and start to close her door.

"Mark, can you stay with me?"

"It's time for bed, Fern," I say.

"Just for a little bit. I'm scared I'm going to have nightmares."

"You won't have nightmares," I say, wanting to go practice. "Look, your light's on and you're sleeping with Mr. Fox."

"Please."

Fern isn't going to budge. I walk over and sit next to her on the bed and pick up Mr. Fox. He's wearing Grace's scarf, so I can't help but smell him. Grace's scent is still there, but it's mixed in with Fern's. Soon it will be all Fern.

"Can you lay with me?" She scoots over. I sigh, but I lie down next to her and Fern puts her head on my shoulder.

"Just for a couple of minutes," I say.

"When Mom and Dad die, I'll be very sad."

Fern brings up death a lot since Grace died. Dad and Jenny say it's her way of working it out. We are supposed to answer her questions as if it's perfectly normal for a six-year-old to be obsessed with death.

"If I die, will you be sad?" she asks.

"Yes," I say. "We will all be sad."

"You'll probably die before me."

Her comment is a little unnerving, but logical. I'm older. Not that age matters. Look at Grace. Seventeen. Way too young. She should have lived to eighty-nine. "Maybe."

"How old is Isabel?" Isabel is Fern's hamster, which she's had for at least a year.

"One."

Jenny looked up the life expectancy of hamsters and it's around three years if you feed them and keep them well. Isabel has been treated like a queen, with water, food, and regular cage changes, and a large wheel she runs on all night.

"When she dies, can we have a funeral for her?"

"If you want."

"Do you ever miss Grace?" she asks.

"All the time."

"Me too. I miss how she used to play with my hair."

"How'd she do it? Like this?" I take a couple of strands of her hair and run it though my fingers, but some catches and I accidentally pull at it.

"Not as hard," Fern says. "More like this." Fern takes my hand and shows me.

"Do you think Grace is in Heaven?"

I don't know. "Yes."

"You think she misses us?"

Where are you, Grace? Do you think about us? "Yes."

"Good."

"Did you know that Grace always wanted a sister?" I ask her.

"She did?"

I nod. "The night you were born we were all at the hospital, waiting and waiting. You took forever to come."

"I did? Why?" I know Fern has heard this story before, but there's something in the telling. Like when she wants you to read her a story she's heard over and over again. She acts like she's hearing it for the first time.

"I guess you wanted to make sure we were all ready for you. After you were born, we went and saw you in the nursery with all the other newborn babies. Grace picked you out right away. She pointed at you and said, 'There she is. There's Fern.'"

"How'd she know it was me?" she asks, a little breathless with wonder.

"She said you were the most beautiful baby. She was so happy to get a little sister."

I was been indifferent when I heard Fern was going to be a girl. I wanted a little brother, but that's not how it went. I didn't like the idea of being outnumbered by females in the house. Grace used to dress up Fern like she was her own personal living doll. Jenny let her because she thought it was so cute.

Fern snuggles close to me. It's not so bad being an older brother. I play with Fern's hair until she falls asleep.

Twenty-One

'm parked across the street again, but the man doesn't come outside. I know he's home. His car—his *new* car—is in the driveway. It's a good choice for a family, one of those Ford wagons. Another car pulls up, and the mom gets out. She pops the trunk and starts unloading groceries. I wait to see if he'll come out and help her. He doesn't. She loses her grip on one of the bags, and I reach for my door latch. I almost open it. To do what? Run out and help her? And then what? At least it would get me across the street and to their door.

I've thought about how things could go down. It involves me knocking, and him answering. His eyes go wide in recognition. It's important that he recognizes me, that he knows who I am. Then I start hitting him, just going to town. I rub my knuckles, imagining the feel of his face and teeth cutting into them. The wife is screaming. The kids—and this is where I always have trouble—as soon as the kids see me, I back away, ashamed. I wasn't counting on the kids. I didn't know how to get them out of the equation. So I come here and sit.

I open Grace's journal. I pretty much carry it with me now. I've been reading it slowly, trying to make her words last.

I've been talking to Mom lately. It started with me calling her to ask if I was shy as a little girl, and then she called me back, and then I called her. We even text sometimes.

I don't know if we'll ever be superclose, but I'm beginning to understand some things I didn't before. Is this what it means to get older? Becoming mature? Trying to listen or to walk a little in another's shoes?

I didn't know Grace was back in contact with Mom like that. I think of my conversation with Dad over lunch and how my running from Mom is making it everyone else's problem. I text Mom to set up a dinner, and I'm surprised at the relief I feel when the date's set. I start the car. I'd better get going if I want to make it to the poetry reading.

· · · ·

The line to the club curves like a cat's long tail. I hadn't expected such a turnout. With the crowd and the excitement, you'd think we were going to a movie premiere or some hot concert, not an open mic poetry session. I get in line, keeping my head down. I don't know if Sebastian and Hanna are inside yet or somewhere in line. I don't want them to see me. I know we're not speaking and I blew it with them, but I need to do this. I need to see the list through. The line moves slowly toward a huge black guy, who looks more like a bouncer for a club than a poet. I'm expecting him to check my ID, but he opens his hand for the cover charge. I give him a five-dollar bill.

I follow the people down the steps, inching my way to the source of the loud hip-hop music emanating from inside. We enter a small theatre with a stage and probably one hundred stadium seats. Most of the seats are already taken. I spot one in the back corner and make my way toward it. I'm not about to join the people sitting on the stage on beanbags, chairs, or the floor. I spot Hanna and Sebastian in the front row. I pull up the collar of my jacket, as if that'll help disguise me, not that they'll be looking for me. They probably don't care if I show up or not. The crowd is urban, definitely more of a hip-hop/rap scene, not your white, beret-wearing, finger-snapping poetry crowd. Most everyone is black, so I kind of stand out being the only Filipino that I can see, but I'm also at home because of the beats.

The DJ spins real vinyl from a far corner of the stage. The mix is early '90s rap, which gives the space a gritty feel. As if he's heard my thoughts, the DJ throws some Public Enemy into the mix.

A black guy with a shaved head, vest, and skinny tie jumps onstage and introduces himself as the host for the night. Everyone applauds. He starts to go through the rules about breaks and conduct. He also reminds people that tonight is open mic, not slam night. Be respectful. Be loving. Be cool. The first round of poets is already full, but they have a couple of open spots for the next, so if anyone wants a turn they can see him at the break.

From where I'm sitting, Hanna and Sebastian look like they're together. She smiles up into his face at something he's said. I'm already mad at Sebastian, but I may have to kick his ass for real this time.

The host calls the name of the first poet from a slip of paper. Freddy. Some twentysomething guy jumps up on the stage. He adjusts the mic stand, raising it up to his height.

"Hello. How you all doing?"

"Hello," people yell back.

"This is called 'Love Is the Shit,'" he says, which makes the crowd laugh. He launches into a story about how he fell for a girl, how she cheated and left him. Most of the poem makes fun of her and couples in love, but it ends with how he looks everywhere for that feeling. It evades him, and all he picks up is its scent, like the one hanging around after someone's used the bathroom. I thought the piece was pretty depressing and gimmicky, but the guy gets a standing ovation.

The next poet is a Latin guy who launches into a speech about the government, and the establishment, and how we need to start a revolution or something like that. He speaks so quickly that I can't catch everything he says. It's not a good poem or performance, but everyone claps for him, too.

Next up is a girl who speaks about relationships. Her performance is so sensual. Her voice sounds like a low oboe moaning across the stage. It makes me wonder if they ever have any musical accompaniment for their poets. Another idea comes to me for Pete's show, but then I remember I'm not doing the show anymore.

As each poet performs, I become more tense because I'm wondering when it will be Hanna's turn. I don't know if she's going in the first group or if she's in the second. I'm hoping it's the first so she can get it over with. I'm nervous for her.

After the sixth poet, the MC calls Hanna's name. She climbs the stairs to the stage and stands in front of the mic. She's wearing her good jeans, the ones she wears when she wants to look cute. Her brown hair is down and straightened. Alone on the stage, she looks small, more like a scared girl than a spoken-word artist. She pushes back some of her chunky bracelets and lowers the mic.

"Hi."

"Hi," the crowd says back.

"I didn't write this poem. My friend Grace did. She made this list." Hanna turns away from the mic and clears her throat. "She made this list of things she wanted to do. One of them was to perform a poem. But then she died, so she never got to. I know she loved this place, so I'm kind of doing this for her."

I hadn't known about Grace's connection to the club. I feel a twinge in my gut, and suddenly I'm pissed. I check myself. It's not like I told Grace everything I ever did or wanted to do. But Hanna knowing this piece of Grace makes me feel like Grace had to hide part of herself from me. Why else wouldn't she have told me about the lounge? Did she think I would have made fun of her? And then there were those entries in her journal. She kept it a secret from me that she was talking to Mom. She kept her fears secret. She kept lots of things from me.

The whole audience seems to sit up a little straighter and lean forward after Hanna's introduction. She takes a deep breath and begins to read.

"If I could tell you, I'd start with how I think you look in the morning. It's not all sunbeams and dew and mountaintops. It's more sleepy eyes and messy hair and pillow lines on your cheek from resting so hard.'"

Hanna's voice falters. She stops and stares down at the paper, and I want to run to the stage, to stand with her, but I can't move.

"It's okay, girl," someone says from the audience. "You can do it."

"Take your time."

"Go on."

"We're with you."

They call out with the same rhythm and cadence of a congregation ready to hear the message in church. Hanna looks up and gives a courageous smile before she starts reading again.

"'If I could tell you, I'd start with how I'm feeling. It's not all butterflies and passion and my heart skipping a beat when you walk in the room. I am scared and shy and overwhelmed.'"

As Hanna talks, her voice gets stronger. I close my eyes and listen to the words, and suddenly it's as if Grace is saying them, not Hanna. It's as if Grace is here, with us, speaking to me.

"'I'd tell you not to say those words, the ones you're hiding in plain sight, the ones that will turn kisses and holding hands into promises. I want to say wait.'"

Hanna whispers, "'Wait. Slow. It. Down. I'm not ready.'" She pauses, and we all wait with her.

"'Time is churning, spinning, swirling us into infinity. I want to open my arms, lie on my back, and let the current take me. Close my eyes and not think about what is ready to pull me into the deep, pull me under. I don't want to think of forever and ever and ever. I want to follow where the water leads, which is to this moment.

"'This moment is not forever. This moment is me and you and us in time. This moment I want to tell you everything, but I can't because I am not everything and you are not everything. Not everything needs to be spoken. Because when you or I speak things, they come to be. Our words become worlds where people dwell and live and hurt and laugh, and there's no destroying what our words create.

"'If I could tell you anything it would be that I am here with you now. And that's better than forever, because lots of things can happen between seventeen and forever.

"'So I will simply take your hand, kiss the tips of your eyelids, and walk with you toward tomorrow.'

"Thank you," Hanna finishes.

The audience stands and applauds. Hanna is beaming. The MC lets us know that it's time for a break. It's my chance to get away unnoticed, so I hurry down the aisle. Outside, I double over on the sidewalk. I try to catch my breath, like someone's punched me in the gut.

"Are you okay?" a girl asks.

"Yes. No." I stand up and it's Hanna with Sebastian. The three of us form an awkward triangle. They don't say anything, waiting for me to say something. The night is cold and Hanna rocks back and forth on her heels.

"You were really good," I say finally.

"I messed up on the first part," Hanna says.

"No, it was perfect," I say. "Grace would've loved it."

"Thanks."

I think of Lily's drawing, taped to a wall in my room. "You guys are my best friends. I don't want to hurt you. I don't want to be a porcupine anymore."

"We all hurt people," Hanna says. "We just need to make it right when we do."

"I'm sorry for hitting you," I tell Sebastian.

He nods. "I forgive you."

I smile because it reminds me of the way that Dad would make Grace and me apologize to one another when we were little. Dad said it wasn't enough to say that you were sorry, it was important to also forgive the other person when you were wronged.

"Thanks, man." I turn to Hanna. "I'm sorry. I shouldn't have said those things to you. Forgive me?"

"I forgive you," Hanna says.

Their forgiveness makes me feel like I can breathe again, but I'm not sure where to go from here.

"It'll be okay," Hanna says.

"How do you know?"

"Because nothing lasts forever."

Normally that sentiment would make me sad, but I am grateful for it. I know she means she's not as mad. She's saying I have another chance.

We start walking and our triangle converges into a line, with me in between the two of them. Where we're going, I don't know, and none of us says anything. We walk a couple of blocks.

"I'm hungry," Sebastian says.

"I could eat," I say. I could do anything now that I have my friends back. But I'm cautious. I don't want to mess anything up.

We head toward the fluorescent lighting of a small diner. The hostess tells us to grab any table. We sit in the corner on ripped red leather seats, patched with silver duct tape, talking about the poets we heard and making our own Top Fives. I sneak glances now and then at both of them, glad that, for the moment, the world is becoming right again.

Twenty-Two

We live on the most perfect street for skateboarding. It's like six hundred yards long, all downhill, and there's not a ton of traffic because it's a cul-de-sac at the top, which is where I start and just let her go. Every now and then I get some freaked-out neighbor lecturing me about how I should wear a helmet because if I'm hit by a car, my brains will be splattered all over the road. My bass teacher would probably kill me, afraid I'd break my wrist or something, if he knew. I don't really care, because skating's awesome. The wind presses against your face, and runs through your hair. It's the closest thing to flying. Sure, I've eaten it a couple of times, but that comes with the territory. Sit out if you're afraid to get hurt.

I turn, skidding to a stop right before the street spills out onto a major road, flip the board around, and push it back up the hill. I could go over to the park, but I wanted some speed this morning.

Hanna comes out and sits on the curb, watching me. Though all has been forgiven, we're still working our way back to normal. I wad up the shyness in my gut, and I skate over to her.

"Want to join?"

"I don't skate." She puts one hand on her hip.

She's lying. She does skate. I learned that a couple of days after she had moved in. I was doing some ollies off my wooden ramp and she came over with a board underneath her arm like she had been skating all her life. She started doing ollies and landed each one solid. I got cocky and tried to land a 180, but came down chicken-footed every time. Hanna stopped skating in the ninth grade, but that doesn't mean she can't.

"Chicken?" I ask, pushing my board up the hill, knowing that'll get her.

I wait for her at the top. She's got an old dusty black helmet on her head and carries her board under her arm as years before.

"Seriously?"

"I'm not going to get brain damage if I fall." The straps hang from both sides.

"Here." I help her with the fastener underneath her chin.

"If you're going to wear it, wear it right." The strap's too tight, so I loosen it. I try to ignore her eyes and the way her skin feels against my fingers. My gaze falls to the rest of her, which I also try to ignore, and I step back a bit. "When's the last time you wore this?"

"Two years ago."

"There." I hit her on top of the head like we're teammates ready to take to the game. "Looking good."

"Just one time."

"Ready? Go." I push off and Hanna is right beside me as we zigzag down the hill. I crouch low on the board, which makes me go even faster. Too fast. I'm not going to be able to stop, so I jump the curb and fall onto someone's lawn, rolling a couple of times.

Hanna gracefully skids to a stop at the end of the street and comes over to me. "You hurt?"

I hold up my elbow, where the blood is already oozing.

"Don't be a wimp. Race you." She pushes off on her board.

I jump up and run with mine, throwing it down in front of me before hopping on.

"That's cheating," she says.

"Look who had the head start!"

She picks up her board and starts running up the hill.

"Who's the cheater now?" I call after her.

• • • •

After skating with Hanna awhile, practicing bass, and working on homework, I text Pete that I'm back in. His response: *Practice tomorrow after school.* Then I get ready for my dinner with Mom. Since she's coming from the south and I'm up north, we decided to meet in the middle at a little sushi place she suggested downtown. When I get there, I scan the restaurant, but she's not here. I take a table for two next to the window, which faces a busy sidewalk and gray bank building. I look over the menu, but know what I want. It's pretty much the same thing every time: miso soup, rainbow roll, and tuna hand roll, for starters. I'm a creature of habit.

I people-watch. Downtown offers a little bit of everything. An eclectic group of suits, a cyclist, an Asian couple walking their dog, and two skinny white hipsters walk by. An old man in black baggy clothes, most likely homeless, paces back and forth on a corner across the street. The waiter asks if I'd like something to drink. I glance at my watch and order a Coke.

About halfway through my second Coke I get a phone call. I let it go to voice mail. I finish the drink in one quick gulp, and leave more than enough money on the table to cover my tab. Outside the noise and the smell of the city rush over me. My stomach growls, but I ignore the hunger. I take a walk and play the message.

"Mark, I'm so sorry. I'm not going to be able to make it. I was called back to the hospital. They're short on nurses. This is the first chance I've had to even make a phone call. I'm so sorry. Please believe me. I . . . Well, I'll try to reach you later."

I hang up. I feel taken and it's my fault. I should have known that Mom wouldn't follow through. I laugh and shake my head. *What an idiot.* But this time feels worse than others. Before, I had Grace to help me face the disappointment that is our mom. I never felt completely abandoned because there was solidarity with Grace. She understood exactly how I felt. This time I'm alone.

A text comes in from Lily.

Today it's the way she'd read to me at night.

I keep walking, surrounded by a city of strangers.

I text back.

Today it's that she was my twin and I was never alone.

Twenty-Three

On Thanksgiving Day we go to Tita Christie's, which is way better than being at home. I think none of us wanted to be there for our first Thanksgiving without Grace. All of Dad's side of the family is here: his three sisters, some cousins, and my grandparents. The food is amazing. There's the traditional stuff—turkey, stuffing, mashed potatoes, green-bean casserole—but there's also a Pinoy flair. There's all this Filipino food that makes me nostalgic and sentimental. Opening the door to Tita Christie's and getting hit with the aromas, it's like I'm returning to a home I didn't know I missed.

The aunties sit in the kitchen around the table speaking Tagalog as fast as a train. They grab at me and pull me toward them, giving me hugs and asking me how I am, have I eaten? When am I going to visit them? How handsome I'm getting. Do I have a girlfriend? But then they get ahold of Fern, and I am saved. They start in on how beautiful she is and how big she's getting. Jenny oohs and aahs about all the food and asks for recipes, which makes the aunties love her more. There's steamed *kangkong* with soy sauce and *kalamansi, bagoong*, steamed white rice. Tita Christie's made her *adobo*, which I haven't realized how much I've been craving until I smell it, even though it's different from my mom's. But I don't want to think of Mom, so I grab a fried golden *lumpia* and take it out of the kitchen. On the dessert table, someone's placed *buko* pie and apple pie and flan. I'm in heaven.

Before we eat, my grandfather offers up a prayer. He thanks God for food and family and all the blessings. He also thanks Him for the strength to get through a painful year. He asks for a moment of silence in memory of Grace. If it were just Dad, Jenny, Fern, and me at home, I would get up and go outside, and even though I still feel like the walls are closing in at the mention of her name, I stay where I am. I remember what Greg said about how other people are grieving too. This is important for my grandfather, so I give it to him.

After we stuff ourselves, the men go to the TV room to watch the football game. The women stay in the kitchen, cleaning up and chatting away about who knows what. I'm thankful for sports and for talk of players and how bad or how good the teams are. We stay for hours.

At home, Jenny asks if I want to watch a late-night movie, but I tell her I have to finish composing something. Jenny pouts because Dad already has a book under his arm and is climbing the stairs to their room. She's on her own tonight.

Upstairs, I put in Sebastian's track for the show and play along. I start adding the notes, hearing both the bass parts and the cello in my head. As I play, I can see when the models start walking in. I don't know if it's my good mood from the food or what, but I think it's going to be a great show. I hope Pete is ready with his designs.

The next morning my bed shakes, and I wake to find Fern jumping on the end of it.

"Fern!" I groan. "Get out of here."

"Time to get up," she says. "Time to go tree shopping."

I look at the clock. "It's only seven thirty."

"I know." She starts jumping again. "But we have to eat breakfast, and get ready, and drive, and find the tree, cut it down, and eat lunch, and come put it up, and make hot chocolate, and string the popcorn, and cranberries, and everything." She says it all in one breath, her voice rising with each activity.

I put my pillow over my head, although breakfast does sound good. I'm sure Jenny has leftovers. Even though I ate like a pig yesterday, it's now a new day, and I'm hungry.

"Come on, Mark." She plops down and crawls toward my head. "Please. Come eat breakfast. They won't let us go until you're ready."

"Okay. Okay," I say, throw the pillow and covers off, and grab Fern, tickling her. She squeals until I free her. She darts away from me. I follow Fern downstairs to a plate of scrambled eggs, rice, and leftover *lumpia* from yesterday. Dad has also made a run to the bakery, so there's some *pan de sal*, sweet bread. Billie Holiday's voice is in the background, coming through the speakers.

"Morning, Mark," Dad says as he cuts a piece of cheese, adds it to the bread, and hands it to me.

"Morning," I mumble.

"Fern, did you wake him?" Jenny asks.

"How can you tell?" I ask. My hair is standing up all over the place and I'm in rumpled pj's: a gray shirt and red plaid pants.

"Yep, but I was quiet about it."

"She was jumping on my bed." I poke Fern in the side and she darts away from me.

"She's just excited," Jenny says, but she gives Fern a stern look.

"I know." I start eating.

"This'll help," Dad says, and places a cup of coffee in front of me. I normally don't drink the stuff, but I think he's right.

"You were up pretty late last night," Dad says. "You finish the piece?"

I nod. "Yep. I'm sending it over to Sebastian today and he'll lay the track for the dancers to practice."

"I can't wait to see it," Jenny says. "I would have loved going to a high school like yours. So creative. It's like being inside the movie *Fame*. Everyone dancing around and singing."

"It's not like we're walking around in a musical." I think of Grace and her Gene Kelly obsession. She would have loved the idea of her life being a musical. Rumor is he was a perfectionist, practicing moves over and over again, long after everyone went home, so that it looked effortless. Which is kind of like me, I guess. If I commit to something, I want it perfect.

Jenny sticks her tongue out at me. "Don't ruin my fantasy."

"There's also the orchestra concert," Dad says. "Right? You're still in that?"

"Oh yes, orchestra," Jenny says, her voice all bland and bored.

I have to laugh. Jenny isn't such a fan of the classical music. She comes to all my performances, but she's obviously more excited about the fashion and dance show.

"They moved orchestra to spring. You don't have to come, Jenny," I say.

"Of course I do. I mean, I *get* to come," she teases.

"I'm going to be a singer," Fern announces. "And you can play for me." She belts out the first line to *Annie*'s "Tomorrow."

"Not bad," I say.

"Thank you. Are we ready yet?" she asks, dancing around like she has to use the bathroom.

"Go make your bed and brush your teeth and by the time you're done, we'll be ready to go."

Fern speeds out of the room, and Dad and Jenny laugh. I finish my food, sipping on my coffee, listening to Dad talk about the business. Jenny places some more eggs on my plate without me having to ask. Our words dance around each other shyly at first, as if we're still not used to it being just the three of us. But it gets easier the more we talk, and soon I know it'll be like there were only three of us all along. I glance at Grace's empty chair, and instead of anger, I feel sadness. I miss her. She should be here.

But I pretend I'm not sad, because I don't want to ruin the moment. I used to think it meant I was being inauthentic, but now I think sometimes it's okay to pretend for others, to choose to be happy, to choose not to be sad. It's an act of kindness. Everyone doesn't need to know how you're feeling all the time.

Jenny places her hand on mine and squeezes it, as if she can tell what I'm thinking, then announces that we have ten minutes until we leave or Fern is going to have a meltdown.

"I'm ready," I say.

At the tree farm, Fern is in charge. We follow her around from tree to tree. I'm carrying the saw and get the job of cutting it down when we find one.

"Ooh. This is a good one," Fern says, stopping at a huge, full tree.

"That might be a little tall," Dad says.

"I don't know if it'd fit in our living room," Jenny adds.

Fern walks around it like she's a professional tree inspector. "Yeah, and here's a bad spot." She points to a huge hole she didn't see at first.

She hops over to another one.

"Here it is," she singsongs.

"That's the fattest tree I've ever seen," I say. The tree is almost as full as it is tall, but it's probably only six feet, because it's barely taller than me.

Fern thinks it's beautiful. I spy a small, skinny one that looks as if it hasn't had as much time to grow. Grace would have picked that one. She usually went for the little ones because she felt sorry for them. It probably had to do with the fact that we watched *A Charlie Brown Christmas* every year. She wanted to be like Charlie and dress up a poor, unwanted tree.

"Is this the one?" Dad asks, standing beside the fat tree.

"This is the one," Fern says definitively.

We take turns walking around, assessing the tree.

"It's very thick." Jenny pulls apart some of the branches to look at the trunk. "And healthy."

"This is it," Fern says again. "Mark, saw it down."

I look to Jenny and Dad. Even though we all get an opinion, we know who really has the authority.

Dad says, "All right, the expert has spoken. Mark, do the honors."

I bend down, and it takes me some effort to saw through the thick trunk. I'm wearing a flannel underneath my jacket because I guess I was hoping for cold weather, but it's seventy-five degrees out. I'm sweating by the time I'm done and have sap all over my hands. Dad takes the top end, I take the bottom, and we carry the new Christmas tree over to the guys at the entrance so they can wrap it up. Once it's strapped on the car, we drive over to our usual restaurant and have some lunch.

I help Dad set up the tree in front of our big living room window, where it always goes. Jenny starts popping the popcorn. When she was a kid they strung a garland of popcorn and cranberries to put on the tree, so she makes us do it too. It's my least favorite part about putting up the tree because I usually prick my fingers. This time I'm prepared, and Jenny laughs when she comes into the living room with the bowl, sewing needles, and thread to see the Band-Aids I've strapped to my fingertips like eraser tops on pencils.

"Mark, a little extreme, don't you think?"

"I'm not taking chances with these." I wiggle my fingers. "They're my moneymakers."

I grab one of the needles and a long piece of thread. "So, Jenny, what're you up to?" I say in a high voice like I'm one of the girls at a knitting party, because I feel kind of ridiculous. I cross my legs to mock her even more.

"Well, Mark, let's see. Work is going well. I have a new client who wants me to design a website for a new restaurant she's opening. And what about you, Fern?"

"I am writing a story," she says. Fern is a little young still for stringing the popcorn, so she is helping Dad remove ornaments from their packaging and lay them on the floor in a straight line.

"What's it about?" Jenny asks.

"A whale that got its tail stolen by a witch."

"Oh, that sounds scary," Dad says.

"It isn't really. Well, parts are, I guess. In the end the whale gets it back and they become friends."

"Want me to make some hot chocolate?" Dad asks.

"Sure, honey," Jenny says.

"Yes!" Fern says.

"Are we ignoring the summerlike conditions outside?" I ask.

"It's not about the weather," Jenny says.

There's a knock on the front door and Jenny yells, "Come in!"

Hanna opens the door wearing jean shorts and a white T-shirt, verifying my previous statement. "Ooh, great tree," she says.

"Thanks!" Fern says.

"Can I help?" she asks.

Jenny hands her another needle and thread, and Hanna sits next to me on the couch. I try not to look at her bare legs, which are touching mine, but it's kind of impossible. Every time she moves, her shorts ride up just a little higher.

"Ouch." I prick my finger through the Band-Aid. I take it as punishment for not being a gentleman.

Hanna laughs. "It's not difficult, Mark. Geesh. Don't be a baby."

"Hi, Hanna," Dad says when he enters the room with a tray of cups. "You want some hot chocolate?"

"Thank you, Mr. Santos."

"I can't believe we're already putting up the Christmas tree," Dad says.

"I know," Jenny says. "This year it kind of crept up on us."

"We didn't even go apple picking," Fern says, a little surprised, as if she's just realizing it.

"No, not this year. Next year, though," Jenny says.

We're quiet for a moment. All of us thinking about how much Grace loved this stuff: apple picking, Thanksgiving, decorating the tree. Grace isn't with us, but in a strange way, her absence makes her even more present.

Fern unwraps an ornament that's a green Christmas tree with a picture of Grace in the center of it. It's the kind of ornament that you make in elementary school, and the kind you beg your parents not to keep putting up year after year. There are a couple of me somewhere in the decorations box too.

"Look at Grace," Fern says. She holds the picture like it's one of her precious dolls.

I laugh. "She hated that picture." It's of her in the third grade. She's got this horrible bowl cut and is missing her two front teeth. She looks like a vampire.

"Remember how she was always putting it toward the back of the tree?" Jenny asks.

Fern gives Dad the ornament. He takes a moment to gaze at it before putting Grace's picture front and center. "I think this was the infamous scooter year," Dad says.

"Sounds mysterious," Hanna says. She's already halfway through her thread. I have more broken pieces of popcorn scattered on the floor than I've actually strung.

"Dad," I cut him off. Hearing embarrassing stories with the family is one thing, but having Hanna here for them is another. She doesn't need any more ammunition to pocket for later use.

"The twins were in third grade, right, Jenny?" he asks as if I'm not in the room.

"Um, I'm right here," I say. I blow on my hot chocolate before taking a sip.

"Yep, third grade," Jenny says. "It was the first year we were together."

"They wanted scooters. So I got Grace a silver-and-pink one and Mark a silver-and-blue one, because I'm thinking, boy and girl, you know, blue and pink. Well, Mark took one look at Grace's scooter and he wanted it. But Grace didn't want to trade, so Mark cried about it."

"He cried?" Hanna asks.

"Slight exaggeration. I didn't cry," I protest.

"Oh, there were real tears," Jenny says. "Your father had to pull Grace aside and pay her off so she'd trade with Mark."

"You paid her?" I ask Dad. "How much?"

"Never mind." Dad lifts Fern so she can add an elf ornament near the top of the tree.

Hanna laughs. "So you were into pink, huh? That's okay. It's a manly color now."

"Shut up," I tell her.

"I have a pink sweater you can borrow sometime," she continues, bumping me with her shoulder. She ties the end of her thread to Jenny's and starts a new one.

"I'll keep that in mind," I say, and bump her back. "And slow down, you're making me look bad."

"Remember when Grace wanted to make the cookies for Santa, but she put salt instead of sugar into the batch?" Jenny asks. "Mark told her Santa would never come back to our house if we left them out."

"You're so mean," Hanna says to me.

"What? They were terrible." They were. I thought all the remembering might make me upset, but it doesn't. The memories flow like water, and I didn't even know how thirsty I was.

"Can I make cookies?" Fern asks.

"Yes, sweetie. I'll help you," Jenny says.

"Grace loved Christmas, didn't she?" Dad says. "Remember last year when she made us all go caroling?"

"That was so fun," Hanna says.

"When she was little, Grace used to sit on my lap before bed and we'd watch the lights on the tree," Dad says.

"Like I do sometimes?" Fern asks.

"Yes, just like you," Dad says.

"One year I remember her telling me that I wasn't getting anything for Christmas because she had gotten ahold of Santa's naughty list. She said I was number one," I said.

"You *were* pretty naughty," Jenny says. "Tracking in dirt, climbing on all the furniture and jumping off, taking all my Tupperware to collect bugs, getting Grace to follow you on all your adventures . . ."

"It wasn't all me! I just wasn't as smart as Grace. She had you all snowed."

We continue decorating the tree, remembering different Christmases and sharing good memories of Grace. I throw in a few that reveal her bratty side just for good measure. It's like we've been given unspoken permission to talk about her freely for the first time since the accident, maybe because the holidays are usually a time to remember.

When we're done with the tree, Jenny puts on the movie *Elf*, another family tradition. It feels good to be together, laughing at stupid jokes and a man-size elf trying to find his place in the world.

Dad sits next to Jenny, one arm around her, the other holding his cell, to check e-mails and messages from work. He's not one of the district managers for nothing. He looks up at the screen and laughs when Buddy is singing. Dad's belly laugh is infectious. I join in, along with Jenny, Fern, and Hanna, the sound of our laughter rising and filling the whole house.

Twenty-Four

You can see all of LA from where we're standing in front of the Griffith Observatory. The distant city lights stretch for miles all around. The downtown skyline is outlined in the distance. In the opposite direction, the HOLLYWOOD sign stands. We're early, but I have some unfinished business before we begin. I know Hanna and Sebastian have questions, but they're being patient. They follow my lead and wait for me to tell them why we're here.

"It's amazing," Hanna says beside me.

"Ever been inside the observatory?" Sebastian asks.

She shakes her head.

"How long have you lived in LA? Come on. I'll give you a quick tour." He holds out his arm.

Hanna looks at me, and I tell her to go. She loops her arm with his and they leave. I've been here before with Sebastian. He comes frequently with a club he's part of.

I'm sitting down at the base of the huge Astronomers Monument when I see River walking up from the parking lot. I wave at him and he heads in my direction.

"Thanks for coming," I say, and stand when he reaches me. I'm not sure how he's going to react, since the last time we were together I was pummeling his face.

"I was curious." He stuffs his hands in his pockets and looks around. "It's different here at night." He adds as if to explain, "I work out on the trail that comes up here when I want to do hills."

I decide to just go for it. "Look, I want to say that I'm sorry. You know, about how I acted at the funeral and everything."

"That was . . . It was a terrible day."

"I shouldn't have hit you."

"You were upset. I get it."

"Still, it wasn't right."

"No . . ." He looks down at his feet, which are toeing at the grass, making a little hole.

I pull the bracelet from my pocket. "We got this package in the mail the other day." I don't bother telling him it was more than two months ago. "The police department sent us a box of

Grace's things from the night of the accident. It was lost, so that's why we didn't get it sooner. Anyway, this was inside." I hand him the bracelet.

He takes it and closes his fingers around it. "She never even wore it." He smiles. "I don't know what I was thinking. I'd never bought anyone jewelry before. My sister helped pick it. I think it freaked Grace out."

"Maybe a little, but she— Here, I think this'll say it better than I can." I hand him a copy of the poem that Hanna read at the club. I don't know for sure if it is about River, but I think it is.

He reads it and starts to hand it back to me, but I tell him to keep it. He folds it carefully and pockets it.

"I loved her," he says. "Maybe you think that's stupid, but I really loved her."

I believe him. "It's not stupid." He looks like he probably still loves her. I wasn't ready before, but now I'm ready to share Grace. She never was mine alone.

"Grace used to send me like forty texts a day. Just little things. Sometimes funny. Sometimes just saying hi. After the accident I couldn't believe she was gone. I'd pick up my phone all day, during class, walking, right after practice, expecting her to text me. But the texts just stopped. That made it seem so real. I scroll down and read her old messages sometimes."

"I lied to you at the funeral," I say.

He looks up from the bracelet.

"When I told you she never loved you. It wasn't true. I know she loved you."

River puts the bracelet in his pocket along with her poem. "Thanks, I appreciate you telling me. You didn't have to."

"No, I needed to. Grace would have wanted me to."

"River?" Hanna says, and we turn toward her voice. She walks over to us with Sebastian trailing a little behind. She gives River a hug and looks at me in confusion over his shoulder. "I didn't know you were coming."

"Yeah."

"So I take it we're not here for a little stargazing," Sebastian says. "Not that we'd see much tonight anyway." He looks up at the sky. "Too much smog and light pollution."

"No." I look at the time. "Come on. We're going to be late."

"Late for what?" Hanna asks.

"The service."

The Twinless Twins group is right where Greg said they'd be, over on the other side of the observatory. Greg greets me with a side hug and pat on the back.

"Glad you could make it. I'm Greg," he says to my friends.

I introduce them. He dips into a cardboard box and hands us each a white taper candle. I recognize some of the other participants from bowling, but there are a few I don't know. Ann gives me a wave and Hanna looks at me in wonder. All in all I'd say there are about twenty or so of us.

"Okay, everyone. I think we should get started," Greg says. We stand in a circle and he lights his candle. He then lights the woman's candle next to him. She lights the man's next to hers and so on, until the whole circle is lit up, causing our faces glow softly and change shape with the moving flames of the candles.

"We are all here tonight because we've lost someone special to us. Please use this space to honor and remember. You can say something or just be silent. When everyone's done, I'll close us."

The flame from my candle dances as people take turns sharing. The wax drips down the sides. I let some fall on my fingers and play with it after it hardens. At Grace's funeral, I didn't speak. I kind of regret that now. But at the time, it was as if people were only reflecting on a two-dimensional version of Grace. I wanted to remember all of her, the good with the bad, the beauty with the ugly. I work up the courage to say something.

After a lull, I say, "Grace could be a real jerk." I feel all the shadowed eyes snap in my direction. Hanna even places her hand on my arm, probably thinking I'm going to go off. "I mean, not all the time. Most of the time she was great. But sometimes she was selfish. She liked being right and getting her own way. If she didn't want to do something, instead of coming right out and saying it, she'd manipulate the situation or make you feel guilty. If she was in a bad mood, it was better to stay out of her way. She was also the kindest, most generous person I've ever known. She gave everything away. She was good with people. She wanted to make a difference in the world." I think of her journal and all the stuff I'm learning about her. "I thought she was fearless, but she was terrified to let people really see her or to get too close. She took your food without asking."

River chuckles next to me.

"Right?" I say.

"She used to tell me that she didn't want anything at the drive-thru, but after we'd pull away, she'd start eating my fries. I'd tell her they were *my* fries, but she'd just smile and keep eating them." He laughs. "I forgot about that."

"Grace hated being cold, so she was constantly turning up the heat in the house when our stepmom, Jenny, wasn't looking. She was compassionate and loyal and a good friend." Hanna is crying beside me. "I don't want to remember some warped version of Grace without her imperfections, because she wasn't perfect. None of us are. I want to remember the way she'd scratch me when we fought as kids, or how she slammed the door on me when she was mad, or how I could tell her anything and know she'd never tell anyone. I want to remember the real Grace."

Hanna wraps her arm around me. Sebastian places his hand on my shoulder and squeezes. We listen to a couple more people share. At the end, Greg tells us to blow out our candles. We do so all at once. Standing in the dark, we wait a few moments before silently splintering off and walking into the night.

Twenty-Five

After two weeks of steady practice, you'd think we'd be ready for, or at least further along on, Pete's fashion/dance/music mash-up, but we're not. I'm trying not to stress, but it's not just Pete's grade and reputation that are on the line. It's Sebastian's and my senior performance, too. I know we'll be judged mainly for the music component, but if the show sucks, that'll affect all of our grades.

If our run-through is any indication of how things are going, it's bad: Pete is wearing sweatpants. *Sweatpants.* As if Pete's ever come to school in sweats.

And the set isn't even ready. Pete contacted Krysta to make large cutouts of downtown to try to capture the feeling of being up on the roof. She's still painting them, which means they won't be ready until at least tomorrow. Pete is pressing her for when she'll have them finished, when she breaks down in tears, telling him that all her people backed out and she can't possibly do everything by herself. Krysta lies down on the floor and curls into a little ball. I'm not too worried. She usually gets this way before a show. Pete leaves her there to do her thing.

Another sign that things aren't going well is that it is seven p.m. We've been here since three p.m. and we haven't even had a proper dress rehearsal.

"Okay, listen up," Pete says. "We're going to take a break. Forty minutes. Grab some food. We'll regroup and run it from the top."

The dancers, who are sprawled in front of the mirrors on the other side of the room, untangle themselves from each other and are the first to leave. Sebastian and I stay to rework some of the timing with the music, mainly from where the models switch to the dancers. We need to add a couple more measures, and I don't want to be too repetitive.

"How long do we have?" Sebastian asks Pete.

"All night if we need it." Pete dangles a set of keys. "Mr. Percy told me to lock up when we're done."

This means we'll be here late. I don't mind. We need the time.

After everyone's eaten, there's more energy in the room. We do more of a stumble-through than an actual dress rehearsal, but we're at, like, 75 percent. Not bad for the night before a show. I've seen worse, and in my experience, this is how it usually is with live productions, especially when you're doing an original show. It might be different if we were putting on some tried-and-true play, but this production is all new, so there're lots of unpredictables.

Hours later, Pete brings us together for a little pep talk. Pete has led tons of shows and he knows how to pull the best out of people. Everyone listens to him, even after a grueling process, because he's tough but respectful. You know that he's for you. I've worked with other directors who bully their cast and crew. They don't get the same opportunities at the school that Pete does.

"Okay, that was better, much better. Dancers, excellent job, but not all of you are jelling together, especially in the last movement. Brandon, Sebastian, Mark, the music is great. I want to see my models before you leave. I need to make adjustments to some of your costumes, or you'll be giving the audience a different kind of show."

We laugh.

"We get to run it once more during lunch tomorrow, and then we'll be here to prep for the rest of the day. If any of you need a pass from class, you can see me. I want to thank everyone for working so hard. This is going to be amazing. For those of us who are seniors, this may be one of our last shows together. Hopefully it'll be memorable. Love you guys."

"We love you too, Pete!" One of the dancers shouts, and they all rush him in a group hug, which ends up being more of a group tackle. Dancers.

As I'm putting away my bass, Pete says, "Mark, I need you and Sebastian."

"The sets?" Sebastian asks.

"Bingo."

I look over at Krysta, who at some point during the evening got off the floor and is painting a cardboard skyscraper. Her shoulders droop, making her look small and sad. She smiles at us weakly.

I text Jenny, asking her if it's okay for me to stay late, appealing to her desire to have attended a school for the arts, as if I'm in one of those high school musical movies and my staying all night will save the show. She just sends me a smiley face and tells me to have fun and text when I'm on my way home.

Lily untangles herself from the dancers and comes over to me. She's in some oversize basketball shorts and a shirt. Her hair is piled all crazy on her head, but she still manages to look cool. "Glad you came back," she says.

"Me too. Still think I'm a porcupine?" I ask.

"Probably, but a tame one." She laughs. "We've all got a little porcupine in us."

"Lily!" Pete gives her a high five. "The dance is amazing. Love, love it." His expression turns serious. "How do you think it's going? Anything we need to do to be more prepared?"

"It's good. I spoke to those who need to clean their lines, but overall I think this show is going to rock. You guys need some extra help?" She nods at the unfinished sets.

Pete's eyes widen. "Yes, could you?"

"Of course." She takes out her phone. "Let me call my dad."

Brandon has his cello in hand. "Sorry, guys, I've got to go. Mom's waiting outside at the curb."

"No worries," Pete says. "Get some rest. See you tomorrow."

"Later," he says.

"I'll walk you out," Lily says, and I watch her carry his bag so he can maneuver the cello more easily.

Pete tries to round up as many people as he can to finish the sets, but in the end it's only Sebastian, Pete, Lily, Krysta, and me. I'm not much of an artist, but, thankfully, painting these sets is like painting by numbers. Krysta has brushed paint on each section so we know what color to use.

I get a text from Hanna while I'm on the tips of my toes, turning the sky black.

Sunrise hike this Saturday morning? Running out of time

She's right. It's already December. Our original plan had been to go sometime over Thanksgiving break, but I've been so

bogged down with Pete's show and concert practice and school-
work that there just hasn't been any time.

Yes. When?

Before sunrise, dummy

Ha ha. You coming to the show?

To see you strut the catwalk in tight pants? Of course

I'm not wearing tight pants

Too bad. Later

Later

Hanna should be the one on the runway in the tight pants.
She's got the body and the attitude. I scroll up her texts again
and smile.

"Who's that?" Pete asks from below, where he's kneeling,
painting the bottom of a building.

Sebastian looks over my shoulder before I can get my phone
into my pocket.

"Hanna," he says.

"Hanna," Pete says, his voice singsongy.

"Who's Hanna?" Krysta asks.

"Mark's love," Pete says. Pete's teased me about Hanna forever.
He wants to know when I'm going to be a man and go for it.

I drip some paint on Pete's head.

"Hey!"

"She's no one," I say.

"Someone's sensitive," Pete says.

"Leave him alone. Wasn't that movie horrible in Velazequez's class?" Krysta says, and she and Lily talk about some foreign film they had to watch in their Spanish class.

"Hike this Saturday?" I ask Sebastian, who's busied himself with windows.

"I can't. I have to work. You crazy kids will just have to go without me." He dips his brush into more gray paint.

"You can't get out of it?" I face him, accidentally dripping some black on the floor.

"Mark!" Krysta says.

"Got it." I wipe up the spill with a paper towel.

"No. Dad's going to be at our truck in San Diego, so I have to man the LA one."

"Bummer." Sebastian's been part of Grace's list from the beginning. He should be there.

"Hiking with Hanna, huh?" Pete asks.

I threaten him with the paint again.

"Okay. Okay. I just find it interesting that you're going hiking. This steps beyond the boundaries of the neighborhood. It could even qualify as a date."

"It's not like that," Sebastian says, coming to my rescue. "Can I tell them?"

If Sebastian doesn't say something, Pete will keep teasing.

Now everyone's curious. I'm ready, I think, for others to know. I nod.

He explains Grace's list.

"That's beautiful," Lily says.

"It's a cool way to honor Grace," Pete says.

We're quiet for a few moments, painting our designated spots.

"Things could get interesting up on that mountain," Pete starts in again. *Unbelievable.* "Sunrise. The two of you. All alone. You should have a plan."

"My plan is to fulfill Grace's list." I bring it back to Grace, hoping that'll shut him up.

"I'm just a romantic. Krysta, Lily, help me out here."

"It *is* romantic," Lily says. "Have you ever talked to her, you know, about your relationship?"

There goes Lily being Lily. Blunt. "We don't have a relationship. We're friends. Good friends. Can't a guy and a girl be friends anymore?" Why does there always have to be pressure to change that? Hanna and I just fit. Sure, we fight and piss each other off sometimes, but we always remain friends.

What I am I supposed to say to her? *Hanna, I think you're cute? Hanna, want to hang out sometime?* I picture her face, and I don't see her swooning into my arms. I imagine her laughing.

We are way past the getting-to-know-you stage, when you

try someone out to see if you want to commit. We are already committed. I don't need to know if we can be something more. For now, less is more.

"We're—what's the word? Platonic?"

Pete groans.

Sebastian and Lily don't answer.

Krysta says, "Let's put it this way. You can be friends, sure. But when a guy and a girl are really good friends, I think there's always a little attraction, even if it's not acted upon."

I don't acknowledge anything out loud, but I think that's probably true. I am attracted to Hanna, have been forever, but that doesn't mean we should date. Or does it? What would happen? Would the world spontaneously combust if we got together? What if it didn't work out?

"It's complicated, guys," I say.

This time everyone groans. Lily even flicks some paint up at me.

"Hey! Not by the sets!" Krysta says.

"It's not complicated," Lily says. "Have a conversation. You'll thank us later."

"Doubtful. Anyone else? What about *your* dating life?" I ask Lily. I did take note that she's been more attentive to Brandon during practices.

She shrugs. "Possibilities. That's all."

"Yeah, a possibility named Brandon," says Pete.

"You are seriously a girl," Lily says.

"I'm just observant," he says.

But we're all waiting for her to respond.

"We hang sometimes. That's it." Then Lily offers up this information: "He's serious and sweet and has great arms. Done. Krysta, your turn."

"Ugh," Krysta says. "Talk about dead in the water."

We listen to Krysta's story about a guy she met over the summer who has suddenly stopped calling her. It's one of those nights when everyone shares a little too much and we'll all probably regret it in the morning. By the time two a.m. comes around, the sets are done. We stand back and examine our work. It's a perfect representation of the downtown skyline.

Sebastian says, "I think we're actually going to pull this off."

I don't admit it, but I'm glad Pete pushed me to do this. People coming together to create something new is always inspiring. Pete had the vision, and I'm grateful it was big enough to include me.

"Thanks, Pete," I say.

His hand grips my shoulder.

"You may want to save that until tomorrow."

"If all else fails," Krysta says, "at least we'll have amazing sets."

"And kick-ass dancers!" says Lily.

"And extraordinary musicians," Sebastian adds.

"With hot models." Pete says to me, "Just don't trip."

"Great, no pressure." I'm already nervous about having to do the catwalk. But I bury that fear, because I want to enjoy the feeling that we might pull off something amazing.

The next night, the auditorium is packed. The whole school has come out to support the talent show. Backstage is just as tight. We're divided into sections according to our place in the show. The backstage manager walks from group to group, checking on us, speaking quickly into his headset.

Pete is looking the part of a designer tonight. His long black hair is pulled back into a ponytail, and he's wearing a fitted black vest and jeans with heavy black boots.

I, on the other hand, am wearing something that Pete dubs "fashion forward"—a white mesh hoodie, camouflage tapered pants, and tan work boots with the laces hanging out. It's not bad, except for the fact that you can see my nipples through the mesh and it's kind of cold.

Pete peeks around one of the side curtains to look at the audience and whispers, "You'll never guess who's here."

"Probably not," I say.

"Fred Sylvester."

I shrug.

Pete is incredulous. "He's one of the recruiters from Otis. I'm going to pass out."

I'm impressed. It'd kind of be like someone from Berklee coming to hear me play. Not that anyone would be here. The school is across the country, and I still haven't applied or sent them an audition video.

Pete grabs me by the shoulders. "This has to be amazing."

"It will be. Everyone will do their job, and it'll be great."

Pete motions for our group to huddle up. It's the one time when we get to feel like we're on a sports team. Right before a performance, there's always the huddle. We bend down so our heads almost touch and Pete, who has calmed down and is leading us seriously, says, "Theatre gods, we offer up this piece. We hope you are pleased. Everyone, remember your cues. Have a great time." He puts his hand in the middle of the circle and we place our hands on top of his.

"On three," he says. "One. Two. Three."

"Break a leg," we say in a strong whisper, trying not to disturb what's going on onstage, which as far as I can tell is some sketch about a guy who is trying to ask a girl out on a first date.

When it's our turn, Sebastian walks out alone onto the stage. He turns on his beat machine and begins a rhythm. As he does, people move pieces of the set onto the stage and start placing the city buildings in the background. Brandon is next. He enters and picks up his cello and adds long, haunting brushstrokes. It's such a great contrast to what Sebastian's playing.

Next up is me, and I have to say I'm actually nervous, but I ignore it, suck in my gut, and take the stage. I try to remember everything Pete told me to do. You'd think it'd be easy to be a model on a catwalk, but it's more technical than I anticipated. I want to do a good job for Pete, especially with the Otis guy there, so at the end of the runway, I take my time and even pull up my hoodie and put my hands in my pockets. It must look good, because I get a lot of yells and applause. I recognize Jenny's and Hanna's voices and feel the flush coming up my neck. I try to coolly walk over to where my bass is waiting next to Sebastian.

I stand behind the bass and start plucking, playing a counter rhythm to what Sebastian's doing. By now a couple more models have started walking the runway. When the last model has done her thing, I give the guys the signal and all the music cuts out. The audience starts clapping because they think we're done. I wait a couple of beats before I start playing. It's a melody that came to me after Thanksgiving.

It was late, or rather early—four in the morning early—and I was tired of tossing. I got this memory of Grace and me. It wasn't anything special, just a night when we were at home together, watching Fern. Nothing looked good on TV, and we were bored. She found a deck of cards, so we decided to play a game of War. I got out a tub of our favorite ice cream, salted caramel chocolate. We played for a good hour. In the end, she may have beaten me, or maybe I beat her? I couldn't remember, but I did remember how happy I was just hanging out with her. That was the feeling I tried to conjure with my bass.

Onstage I close my eyes and I can see Grace, sitting across from me at the table. Her long hair frames her face and she's chewing on a stray piece. She's humming as she looks at her hand of cards. I try to put that humming into my bass, moving the bow slowly across the strings, capturing the low alto of Grace's voice.

I open my eyes just as Lily steps out and starts dancing. Her movements are slow and stretch across the stage, becoming a visual representation of what I'm playing. Sebastian adds a hip-hop rhythm. Lily looks to the right and then the left, and as she does, the other dancers enter. Brandon comes in with the voice of the cello, and I start plucking. The mood changes, becoming more upbeat, more tribal.

I signal for the last count, and after the final note resonates, the audience goes crazy. They give us a standing ovation. The dancers take a bow, followed by the models, and then the musicians. The last one to come out is Pete. He runs up and bows, then joins all of us in a line and we all bow again. You'd think we just completed a Broadway show.

I look out and see Dad, Jenny, Fern, Hanna, and Hanna's mom in the audience. They've all got big smiles on their faces. I imagine Grace being there, right next to Hanna, cheering just as loud.

"You guys were so good," Jenny says, and hugs me. I pat her a little on the back.

"Your piece was compelling," Dad says. "Never would have thought to combine orchestral variations with hip-hop. Well done, Mark."

"Thanks, Dad."

"Not bad," Hanna says. She also hugs me. I untangle from her quickly, feeling awkward in front of everyone, not that I have anything to feel awkward about. We've hugged as friends forever.

"Loved it," Hanna's mom says.

"Thanks, guys."

I see Pete on the side of the stage talking to some man I don't recognize. They're shaking hands. It must be the guy from Otis. From what I can tell, Pete will have no problem getting in.

"Mark?" I recognize the voice before I turn. She stands with her hands folded in front of her. Her hair is longer than the last time I saw her.

I don't say anything and it gets uncomfortable, like being in a too-hot room. Dad and Jenny say hello and something about being happy she came. I didn't tell my mom about the show, so they must have. Betrayed by my own family. I need to get out of here.

"I've got to take care of my bass," I say, and walk away, but I don't go to the stage. Instead, I head outside. I look around, but where am I going to go? I sit on one of the benches.

"Mark," Mom says as she approaches me. "Can I sit down?"

I shrug, but move over to give her room.

"When you were little, you looked so tiny playing your bass. You loved it. You'd spend hours. . . . I knew you were good, but I had no idea how good."

I study the ground.

"I'm so sorry about dinner," she says. "I know that doesn't fix it, but I'd like to take you out tonight. I'll make it up to you."

"I have plans."

"Mark, I'm trying here—"

"It's a little late." I cross my arms protectively, determined not to let anything she says penetrate.

"I know. I said I was sorry about dinner."

"This isn't about the stupid dinner," I say. "This is about how you just left us. I mean, what kind of mom leaves her kids? You didn't even look back. For years you didn't want anything to do with us. And now—now I'm supposed to be all happy that you want to be in my life? I'm supposed to just forget? It doesn't work that way." I stand up. I know I'm being disrespectful and Dad will be upset, but I don't care.

"You're right," she says. "Please don't walk away. Please."

Something in the way she says "please" makes me hesitate. Her voice rises a little in the end, the way Grace's used to when she really wanted me to do something. I sit back down.

"You're absolutely right. It was horrible what I put you and Grace through. There's no explanation or excuse I could give that will take that away. But I would like to say something if you'll listen."

I stare at the ground, so she keeps going.

"I was in a bad place. I know that now, but at the time, I couldn't think clearly. I felt trapped by everyone and everything. I was terrified I was going to do something awful to you, to myself. My only option, I thought, was to leave. I convinced myself that I was sparing my family, that it would be better for you and Grace—and even your dad—if I left. I was broken. I eventually found a therapist who helped me work through some of my issues, but by then, there was this strain between us. I didn't want to cause any more damage, so I stayed distant."

"I was just a kid," I say, remembering how Grace and I would hold each other at night, wondering what we'd done to make Mom so mad that she left.

"Oh, Mark." Her voice catches. "I have so much regret. So

much regret. I wish I had done things differently. I wish I could take away all the hurt that I've caused. I wish I were a better mother to you and Grace, or even a decent one. I always thought I'd have more time. I'd tell myself that I'd explain when you were older. That you'd understand that sometimes we come to the end of ourselves and it takes courage to find our way back.

"But then Grace died and the illusion that you can always do something tomorrow was shattered. Though we did connect a little in the end, I never got the chance to make things right with Grace. That's something I'll always live with. But I'd like to see if we can move forward. I'd like you to give me another chance."

My first inclination is to leave her on the bench, alone and hurting like she left me all those years ago. It would be good payback. But Mom wanting to make things right, I get that. I've caused my share of pain. It's the worst feeling. I remember how good it felt when Sebastian and Hanna forgave me for being such a jerk.

I wish Grace were here. I wouldn't have to shoulder so much on my own. I could follow her lead. But she's not. There's only Mom and me and the quiet sitting between us.

Mom's eyes are on her hands, clasped together on her lap. They remind me of Grace's hands. They're small but surprisingly strong. When I was sick, Mom would place her hands on my forehead. They felt so cool against the heat of my head. She'd tell me stories of giants and dragons. She called me her little prince. Sometimes she'd sing me a lullaby called *Uyayi*, which she said her mom sang to her, until I'd fall back asleep. Even now I can hear her voice, faded like a memory you are uncertain was real or part of your imagination.

Matulog ka na, bunso (Sleep now, youngest one)

Ang ina mo ay malayo (Your mother is far away)

At hindi ka masundo (And she can't come for you)

May putik, may balaho. (There's mud, there's a swamp)

I don't have the words to say to her. They'll have to come later. There will be a lot for us to work out. You can't fix a lifetime of hurt in a couple of minutes. But I can do something. I reach out and place one of my hands over hers. Mom's body shakes a little and she clasps one hand over mine. It's cool and soft like I remember.

Twenty-Six

At 5:01 the next morning, I watch Hanna open her front door, zip up her jacket, throw a bag over her shoulder, and walk across the street to where I'm waiting with my car already running. I point to the time on my dashboard when she's settled in the front seat.

She groans. "Don't start. You're pulling a Sebastian."

I laugh. "Is that what we're calling it now?"

She puts her feet up on my dashboard and laces her sneakers.

I point at them. "Really?"

"Oh yes, the sacred new car. Just think of it as me breaking it in. What is that smell? I'm going to get a headache." She rips off the little tree hanging from my rearview window and throws it onto our lawn.

"Wow. You're really not a morning person."

"Shut it. I'll pick it up later."

"Okay. No talking." I turn on the stereo and a Mozart sonata I'm working on for school fills the car. I move to change it, but she says, "This is nice."

We drive the ten minutes to the base of the mountain trail with Mozart guiding our way. Everything is dark and quiet. The freeway is empty, which feels kind of ominous because when is the freeway ever deserted in LA? But it's also peaceful. I glance at Hanna out of the corner of my eye and her scowl is gone. Her head leans against the window and her features are soft, as if she's going to fall back asleep.

I park alongside the road near the entrance to the trail and get out. I adjust my beanie and button up my jacket. I wish I'd brought gloves. I show Hanna the two water bottles that I brought for us, which I offer to carry. She stuffs her bag underneath the front seat of the car.

"All right. Let's do this thing!" Hanna says, all smiles as soon as she's out of the car.

"Did you take your happy pills?"

"The music. It always sets me right."

I know what she means. I love all kinds of music, even a little country, though I would never admit it. But classical music takes me to another place entirely. It's probably because I've studied so much of it.

I lead us on to the path with a flashlight guiding our way. We walk side by side along the narrow trail, brusquely, heads down, fronting the cold.

"So, you want to talk about it?" she asks.

"What?"

"Last night. Your mom."

"Oh, that. She wants me to give her a chance."

"Wow." Her voice is full of concern. "What'd you say?"

"I told her I'd think about it."

"Really?" Hanna glances at me sideways, probably surprised because she knows the history.

"Not in those words."

"How do you really feel about it?" She asks the question like she's choosing her words carefully. I want to tell her she doesn't have to tiptoe around me. I offer the truth.

"Weird. But I'd like it if I weren't so angry anymore. No matter what, she is my mom. I can accept that she's different now and sorry for what she's done, but it's not like you can go back in time and change what happened."

"Unless you're a terminator."

I'm thrown off and kind of impressed. "You've seen *The Terminator*?"

"It's a classic. A little dated with cheesy music and acting, but the concept still holds up. Sebastian made me watch it with him in exchange for his help with chemistry," she confesses.

Figures. The Terminator movies are in Sebastian's canon of SF films.

"Well, time travel could never work anyway," I say. "Too many paradoxes."

"That's only if you see time as linear. It's kind of like the multiverse thing. You have to think of time as cyclical."

I stop and stare at her. "Wow, you and Sebastian did get close while I . . . you know."

"While you were being Jerk Mark?" She keeps walking.

I catch up to her quickly, wondering if I should apologize again and if Sebastian helped her with anything else. It's good they're becoming friends, but I don't want them to get *too* friendly. He was there for her at a time when I clearly wasn't, and I can't change that, but I can make sure I'm the one who's there for her in the future.

"Um, yeah," I mumble. "I said I was sorry."

"I know, Mark. I'm just teasing."

"If you're still upset, I understand. You can tell me." My voice is shaky.

"We're good."

Relief sinks in, though I still feel on edge. There's a conversation I need to have with her, but I don't know how to begin.

"Besides, that's only if you go back in time," she says. "What if you could travel to the future? Then there's no problem with changing the past."

"Except you're changing the future." I can stay here, safe within the context of the time-travel conversation. It's easier than discussing our relationship.

"Well, that's only if you believe events are predetermined. You know, fate and destiny and all of that. Is it going to be uphill the whole way?" Hanna sounds winded already.

"Yes, but it switchbacks, so it's not in one long hill at least."

"Switchbacks or not. This sucks." She sighs loudly. "How many miles is it?"

I ignore her whining. "I like the idea of fate, but I don't think it's real. It's a cop-out. It's the word we use when we can't explain something or when we want to give up our responsibility. We choose the life we live."

It's true. Even though Grace was taken from me, I still have the choice about how I'm going to live. I don't believe it was her destiny to die at seventeen. I believe a man made a bad decision. The consequence was that Grace lost her life. And her death affects all of us. But it wasn't fate. My life isn't mapped out for me. I can choose how I want to live. I can choose to be angry or not. Or I can choose to love. I look at Hanna, but she's focused on the path.

"Maybe it's kind of like having that feeling you're doing what you're supposed to be doing, like when you play the bass or when I organized the food drive last year at school, you feel good. No, more than good. You feel like you are supposed to be alive. Maybe that's fate. My head hurts." She touches her temple. "Can't we just think of puppies?"

"Puppies?"

"Yeah. Puppies are perfect. They're so cute. Puppies love you, no questions asked. When you come home and they see you, their whole bodies shake with joy."

"Too bad they grow up to be dogs."

She sticks her tongue out at me. "Is it safe out here?" Hanna asks.

I look around at the mountain and thick bushes that frame the trail. Because of her question, I suddenly have that feeling that we're being watched. I don't let us stop. If we do, we'll probably hear all kinds of things moving in the gray. "Why? You see something?" I point my flashlight in the direction she's looking.

"No, it's just dark and we're by ourselves."

"It's getting lighter." It is. A faint fluorescent bluish light is just beginning to creep into the night, ready to make it day. I don't even really need the flashlight anymore.

"You know what I mean. There could be a serial killer or something out here."

"Yeah, you know, all of those serial killers who love hiking in the early morning hours."

"Or weird people. Weird hiker people. People living in tents. People living off the land, the off-the-grid types." She is frightening herself, so I give her a little pat, but she hangs on and loops her arm through mine.

"You guys were amazing last night, by the way," Hanna says, changing the subject.

"Thanks." I pull her closer to me because I don't want to take any chances and have her stumble toward the edge. We're pretty far up, and peering over the cliff, I see a fall from here would be deadly.

"I'm going to say something serious," she says. "I'm just preparing you."

I'm suddenly concerned, though Hanna has done this to me before and then said something like, "I don't like thin-crust pizza." I still brace myself for what she has to tell me. Maybe she's going to bring up the subject of us.

"You have a gift with music," she says. "I don't know how you do what you do, but you have to keep playing. Maybe that's at Berklee or maybe it's not, but you have to play."

I relax. No talk about defining what is happening with us.

I'm a little disappointed because if Hanna brought it up, it'd force us to have the conversation.

"For a long time I used to think music was about the notes," I say. "But now I think it's more about the intervals *between* the notes. It's easy for me to get lost in it because music is everywhere and when you are listening or playing, you know you aren't alone."

"See, even when you talk about it—a gift."

I take a chance and say, "We should play together some time." It's not asking her on a date, but it's in the right direction.

"Oh no. No way."

"Why not?"

"Remember that one time? You were all upset because I couldn't keep up. Besides I'm not sure how a bass and violin would work."

"It's unconventional, sure, but Edgar Meyer does a lot with the cello and bass; I'm sure we could figure out a bass and violin. Anything could work." I'm talking music, but I'm thinking of Hanna and me. "Most things can, if you want them bad enough."

But Hanna is clueless. "Puppies," she says. "We should just stick to puppies."

We continue hiking, and the higher we go, the more the air feels crisp and clear. The rising sun gives off a little heat. In the summer it can be brutal to hike here because there's no shade and it's so dry that the dirt gets in your mouth. You want to start super early and bring plenty of sunscreen and water, but this time of year it's cold in the morning. It's normally pretty crowded too, but I guess we're here before the crowds. I pass a water bottle to Hanna and she stops in the middle of a step to take a long sip before giving it back to me.

"Okay, so we can see the sunrise from here, right?" she says. "I mean, did the list say that we have to make it to the *top*? Didn't it just say 'hike to see a sunrise'?"

I stand behind her and put my hand on her lower back. "Almost there." I gently push her forward. "This is the toughest part."

I keep talking to distract her. "You'll love it. There's this old railcar at the summit because a long time ago there used to be a huge hotel that people rode up to stay at. The hotel ruins are there too, though just the foundation and some signs with photos. There's an old echo phone—"

"But, Dad, I'm tired," she whines. She leans back into me even more.

"Come on, I can't carry you up." I keep nudging her up the last part of the trail to where it stops climbing and spills onto a wider flat dirt trail. "Keep moving. See, there's what's left of the rail." I point to the rusted tracks and remains of a car. There're weeds growing up through the wheels. I maneuver her around some boulders and then out to a flat ridge that overlooks the valley of houses spread out below us like a scene from a postcard.

We've arrived just in time. As the orange light leaks from behind the San Gabriel Mountains, the sky catches fire, with brilliant reds and oranges igniting all around us. It's like a canvas and some unseen artist is adding new layers with each second. Say what you will about the smog, it gives LA some amazing sunrises and sunsets.

"Wow," Hanna whispers.

"Wow" doesn't even cut it. I've seen sunrises before, but never from this high. The perspective gives a clarity that you can't get from the ground. I am so small, like an ant on a hill. Watching the sky burn, I think of how the sun rises every day no matter what is happening below. No matter who is getting up early to go to work, no matter what work is being done, no matter what fights people are having, no matter what happiness, or sorrow. Life keeps going.

Maybe because Hanna's standing with me or because I've lived through something terrible that I never thought I'd find my way out of, but the thought doesn't depress me. It makes me realize I'm a part of something bigger than myself. As long as I'm alive, I'm underneath an endless sky, on a planet in a solar system that's lodged within a massive universe.

As the warmth of the sun hits my body, every cell within me is yelling, "I exist! I am here!" That's not something to waste. Hanna shifts her body next to me. I'm not alone, and that gives me hope.

"Want to say anything?" I ask Hanna, knowing she probably will.

"Grace, I hope you like your sunrise."

We watch the colors morph and continue to change the sky.

"Come on," I say. "Let's use the echo phone."

"What's that?"

"There's a natural echo across the canyon, over there." I point to the mountain on the other side of us. "They put up a phone that you speak into and your voice carries even more." I lead her to the brown device, which is about Hanna's height. It's a very simple contraption, just a straight metal base and a funnel at the top, like a megaphone.

I think about what to say, and shout, "Hello!" into the mouthpiece. Yes, very clever. In a couple of seconds my voice echoes twice from across the canyon.

"Grace!" I yell into the echo phone. Her name reverberates against the rock walls three times before it fades from our hearing. I picture the sound traveling until it reaches her.

I look back at Hanna and she's holding her temple with her hand.

"You okay?"

"Yeah." She shakes her head as if she's trying to wake up.

"Just a little light-headed. What should I say?"

"Whatever you want." I step aside.

She puts her mouth to the phone and says, "I miss you." It's not as clear as a single word, but Hanna's voice fills the canyon. Hanna moves back from the echo phone to let me have another turn. I say a bunch of silly things, like, "Cheeseburgers" and "Yo Santos!" and stuff.

"Your turn," I tell Hanna, but she doesn't respond. She's staring into the canyon, and lets out a big yawn.

"No. I'm done."

"We did get up before dawn." I take a drink of water and offer her some, thinking maybe she's a little dehydrated.

"I'm fine," she says with an edge and walks back to the cliff with the view of the valley and sits down in the dirt.

I get this buzzing in the back of my mind, a red flag. "How are you doing? You need something?"

"I wish you would stop doing that. I said I was fine. I'm not a child."

I haven't heard Pepe go off or anything, but Hanna's acting ornery, like she's low.

"I know you're not a kid." I keep my voice calm, so I don't irritate her. "But you seem a little off."

"I'm fine," she says again, but her head droops and she suddenly seems very tired, almost loopy.

Now I'm worried. I've seen Hanna get this way before when she needed something high in sugar quick. "You want to check Pepe for me?"

"I'm fine." She folds her arms across her chest and stares straight ahead.

I try a different tactic. "How about we make a bet?"

"I don't like bets."

"Since when? If I win, you take something. If you win, I owe you twenty bucks." I look around for her bag, then remember she left it in my car. She probably has a protein bar in her pocket.

She pats her side. "Pepe is under control."

I bend down next to her and get close to her face. "Hanna, let me see Pepe."

"No." She holds an arm against her side, shielding her insulin pump from me.

"Please?" I plead. She's getting more difficult, so I know it is serious.

"No."

I remember what her mom had told me about when she gets stubborn, I needed to be firm.

"Hanna, I am going to check Pepe." I place my hand on her arm to move it, and she pouts, but she doesn't give me much resistance. Sure enough, her pump's lower than fifty-five, which

I think is really low. I make her look. "See? I'm right. I win. Not that I want to gloat or anything."

She takes an exasperated breath and glares at me.

"So why don't you eat something, okay?" I use the voice that I use with Fern when she needs a little coaxing. "Let's see what you've got with you. Can you stand up, please?" I help her to her feet. She pats her pockets.

"Oops," she says, and giggles. "I think I forgot."

"What?" I start searching her pockets, even though she's swatting my hands away.

"Hey, stop that."

She doesn't have any food, a sugar packet, or even her glycogen pen, which she usually carries for emergencies. I bet it's all in her bag back in the car. Why didn't she bring it with her?

"Hanna, Hanna, listen to me." I'm level with her now, right in her face, which has gone pale. Her eyes are looking at me but not looking at me. Her pupils are dilated. "Your sugar is very low. We need to figure out how we're going to get it back to normal." I'm trying to be calm for her, but I'm starting to freak out. It's a long way back to the car. There's nothing around us. How are we going to get down the mountain?

"It's not low. Leave me alone, Mark." She staggers away from me.

"Wait," I say. I grab her arm, worried she might get too close to the edge.

She shakes off my hand. "You always do this. Trying to take care of me all the time. You don't know." She waves her hand at me. Small sweat beads are starting to form along her forehead. "And I'm not going to make the cake. I won't do it. It's, I don't know, not a good time. I'm not tired, don't want to go to bed yet, and he is sometimes fun, but sometimes annoying." She's not making any sense. This is bad. This is really bad.

My hand shakes as I dial 911, but there's no service on my phone. I walk around, holding it out, trying to pick up a signal, but there's nothing. We're in the mountains. It's almost impossible to get reception here. I get Hanna's phone from her back pocket. Same. No signal.

Hanna sits back down in the dirt. I can't panic. I won't panic. I know if I don't get her help, she could pass out or worse. Fear grips me suddenly. I can't think of worse. There's not going to be a worse.

"Okay, Hanna. Here's what we're going to do. We're going to get down this mountain." I try to calculate the time in my head. It took us over an hour to hike up. It's probably around two-point-five miles, but downhill we should be able to make it faster. We can even run.

Hanna smiles lopsided as if she's drunk, but at least she

doesn't try to fight me as I help her to her feet, put my arm around her waist, and pull her alongside me. She's mumbling something, but I can't really make it out.

"Let's go."

We start to make our way down. Hanna acts like she's sleep-walking, stumbling more than walking. She's awake but not entirely present. I have to guide her every step.

"This'll be a crazy story we can tell people one day. Just stay with me. You're doing great." As I say the words, Hanna's body goes limp, and I catch her just before she falls. I slowly sink to the ground with her.

"Hanna." I hold her face. Her skin is balmy. Her eyes are closed. I place my head on her chest. She's still breathing regularly and mumbling. She opens her eyes, but she's out of it.

We're completely alone in the middle of nowhere. There aren't even other hikers. My heart is racing and I don't have time to think. I pick her up, cradling her like a child, and start moving as fast as I can down the mountain. The switchbacks are difficult carrying Hanna's weight. My knees buckle as I try to run with her, and I have to slow my pace.

I try to think about something else, anything other than how my arms are burning and my legs are ready to give out. I think of the first time I met Hanna. The day after she moved in across the street from us. Grace was so excited to have a girl her age in the neighborhood. I was disappointed she wasn't a boy, but then she came over with her skateboard. Maybe that's the day I fell for her. Pink helmet, pink-and-green board, knee and shoulder pads. She looked like a skater wannabe. But when she did her first jump off the ramp, she was the real deal.

I look down at Hanna now, head back, mouth open, hair hanging limp. *Not like this. She can't die like this.* My body has broken out in sweat. My pulse is racing too fast, beating so hard it's pounding in my head. I have to stop and rest, laying her down on the ground.

I scream out, "Help!"

This time there's no echo because we're out in the open on the side of a cliff with only brush and rock surrounding us.

I scream again. "Help!"

No one answers. No one is coming for us. Hanna is going to die. I get down next to her on the ground. She's going to die in my arms. Hanna's staring at me. She tries to speak, but it's gibberish. I take out my phone again. I have a faint signal. One bar. I dial 911.

An operator answers. "Nine-one-one, how may I be of assistance?"

"I need help. I've got a diabetic. Her sugar's low. She's in trouble. I'm hiking at Echo Mountain Trail. Can you send an ambulance or something?"

The operator on the line asks for my location again and I tell her. She keeps asking me questions about Hanna's condition as if we have all the time in the world and wants me to stay on the phone with her until help comes. I tell her I can't wait, and I keep the phone on but put it in my back pocket, figuring they can track it or something. I help Hanna to her feet and kind of throw her over my shoulder. I start running down the trail.

Please, God. Please, God. I say over and over in my head. *Not like this. Not again. I'll do anything.* I start making deals, even though I know the chances of God needing to make a deal with me are slim. I still offer anything, everything I have. My car. My bass. *I'll never play music again, or, wait, I'll play for church, every Sunday. Please don't let Hanna die.*

I zigzag back and forth down the dirt trail, ignoring the pain in my knees. Hanna is not going to die. I can do this. I press through the burning and the exhaustion in my limbs. The sun is now up and everything is bright, but my mind takes me to where it is dark.

It's night. I'm upside down in the car. It takes me a few moments to understand what has just happened. We've had some kind of an accident. My head hurts and I reach up to touch the pain. It's wet and sticky with blood.

"Grace?" I say, and turn toward her. She's upside down too, but crunched up, her head touching what was the ceiling of the car, and curved inward toward her chest. Her eyes are open.

"Grace? You okay?"

She doesn't say anything. She just stares. Something about her gaze makes me sick to my stomach. I don't think she's breathing, so I wait a couple of seconds, watching her chest. It doesn't seem to move. I unlatch my seat belt and try opening the door. I have to kick it a few times until it opens and I crawl out and over the broken glass.

"Are you okay?" A man runs toward me. He's bending down in my face. "Are you hurt? I'm so sorry. I didn't even see you." He helps me to my feet.

"My sister," I barely make out.

I push past him to get to the passenger side. Her door is bent and busted as if someone took a huge fist and rammed it into the passenger side of the car. With the man's help, I open it and get inside next to her. She's still looking at something.

"Grace." I unlatch her belt and fall on her.

"Wait. Should you move her? The ambulance is coming." There's fear in his voice, but I ignore the man and keep pulling Grace until she comes free from the car.

"How is she? Help is coming." He yells into his phone, "The Colorado Street Bridge. I don't know. There's two of them. One's not moving."

I sit on the asphalt and hold Grace so she's looking up into my eyes. There's blood, lots of blood oozing from her head. It wets through my jeans where her head rests. I keep waiting, waiting for the breath.

"Is she breathing? Oh God. Oh God. I'm sorry. I'm sorry."

"Grace. Grace, don't leave me." I smooth some of her dark hair from her face, but her eyes are vacant and tell me that she's already gone.

In the distance, I hear sirens. I hug her to me and stumble toward the sound. I break through the bottom of the trail and into the street.

"Help me! Help." I fall onto the asphalt with Hanna, confused for a moment because I thought I was holding Grace.

A couple of EMTs rush up to me and grab Hanna.

"She's diabetic," I force out.

"We got her," one of the EMTs says.

They give Hanna a shot of something right away. As I watch them work on her, I can't slow my breathing. My hands are tingly and I feel light-headed.

My body shakes, as if it's chilled to the bone, but I'm drenched with sweat. I try to ask the EMT who's with me a question, but my teeth chatter too much.

"She's going to be okay," the EMT says, and puts a thin blanket over my shoulders.

Something cracks in the deepest part of me. I try to hold it together, but I'm not strong enough. The feeling rises in my throat. I try to cough it out. My eyes fill and the drops fall, running down my face. I wipe them away, but they keep coming. It's like a dam has been removed. I can't hold them back.

"You carry her all the way down?"

I nod. He sits next to me and pats me on the back.

"You did good. You saved her life. But your body's in shock. You'll come out of it. See this bag? I want you to take some deep breaths for me. It'll help you stop hyperventilating."

I can't hold the bag because my hands are shaking too much, so he holds the bag to my lips. I breathe in as slowly as I can and follow it with a slow breath out. I do this a couple of times and it helps. But it doesn't stop the tears. And the tears make it hard to breathe.

"I'm—I'm sorry," I stammer.

"Nothing to be sorry about. You've been through a trauma. Crying is a way of releasing some of the tension. If you need to—"

I bend over and throw up right on his feet.

"Yeah, I was just getting to that." He pats my back in a soothing rhythm. "That's okay. You're going to be fine. She's going to be fine. You did the right thing. Everything's going to be all right."

The EMT helps me into the ambulance next to Hanna. She's lying down, strapped to a gurney. She moans and opens her eyes. I see she hasn't left me like I feared. The ambulance begins to move, and I remember this scene, but it's Grace on the gurney. I've got a bandage around my head and the EMT is telling me to lie back down, but I'm not listening. I'm telling him to get out of my way, that I've got to get to my sister. Her eyes are closed. Why are her eyes closed? She's got all kinds of tubes in her arms and she's wearing some kind of mask that's too big for her face. I can't see her. He finally lets me hold her hand. It's cold, so cold, but I hold it tightly, warming it with my own. I ignore the smell of the blood that's all over me and her and the ambulance.

Hanna's trying to say something. I move close and take her hand. She smiles at me through her mask.

"You're going to be okay," I tell her.

She's speaking again, so I bend my head toward her.

"Thank you," she whispers.

My forehead touches hers and some of my tears streak her face.

Twenty-Seven

Dad and Jenny come to the hospital. Dad grabs me in a violent hug. Jenny is a little gentler. Their terror and relief almost kills me.

"When I got the call ..." Dad starts but can't finish.

"I know, Dad. I know. I'm okay, just in shock." I tell them about Hanna getting low and me carrying her down the mountain.

"Is she all right?" Jenny asks.

"I think so. She was coherent during the ambulance ride, though we didn't talk much. She rested."

"Proud of you, son," Dad says. He squeezes my arm.

I suddenly have to get out of there. The idea of spending any more time in the ER is too much for me. I keep thinking about the last time I was here. My back was against a wall, blood all over, not wanting anyone to touch me, not even Dad and Jenny when they came rushing up to me, waiting to hear what was happening with Grace behind one of the doors. I couldn't tell them that she was already dead. How could I tell them that?

"Yeah, well, can we go? I've got to go get my car."

"The car can wait," Jenny says. "Want to see Hanna?"

"No," I say. Even the smell of the hospital is getting to me. "I need to leave. It's this place. . . ."

As if my dad gets it, he says, "Sure, of course. Let me clear you with the doctor." He goes to the nurse's desk.

"That must have been scary seeing Hanna that way," Jenny says.

Thinking about Hanna almost dying, I start to feel the pressure build behind my eyes. I shrug, afraid to speak about it because I'll start crying again.

Jenny takes my hand. "Is Hanna's mom here?"

"Yeah, she's with Hanna." Hanna's mom rushed all frantic into the waiting room. She saw me and I told her what happened. Before going to see Hanna, she hugged and thanked me for saving her little girl's life.

Dad returns to us. "We're good to go. You were never admitted or else it'd take forever to check you out. So we can leave, or if you want to say good-bye to Hanna first, we can wait."

"No, I'm good." I can't face Hanna yet. Everything's just too close and jumbled and confusing.

We leave the ER in a chain, with me in the middle and Jenny's and Dad's arms linked through mine. Normally I'd mind all the attention, but today I don't. Today it makes me feel loved and I need that.

Dad drives us back to the trail's entrance so I can get my car. He starts to insist that he drive and I ride with Jenny, but I tell them I'm fine for the hundredth time and that I'd really like to be alone.

They look hurt, so I assure them, "It's nothing personal. I need to, you know, clear my head. Please."

Jenny and Dad exchange a glance.

Dad says, "Keep your phone on." He tries to keep the worry out of his voice, but I hear it.

"Of course."

They pull away, and I sit for a few moments in my car. The street is almost lined with parked cars, a direct contrast to the morning. I can't believe it was only a couple of hours ago that I was parking and Hanna and I were beginning our hike. How quickly everything can change. Hanna will be hurt that I didn't see her in the hospital, even though she knows I hate hospitals. But I push that thought away.

I debate calling Sebastian, but decide not to bother him while he's working. What would he say anyway? Sorry?

I start the car and head over to the bridge. I walk along the path and marvel again at this small piece of nature tucked in between freeways and buildings. It's different during the day: all flowers and gnats and people walking dogs, not shadows and ghosts. I prefer it, though, in the peace of the night when so many cars aren't buzzing by.

I climb to the top and walk along the bridge itself. There's a break in the traffic, so I step off the sidewalk and out into the road. I bend down close to the asphalt.

The stain is still there. The part they missed when the cleanup crew tried to remove it after the accident all those months ago. The spot of blood. Mine or my sister's or both, it doesn't matter whose. We shared the same blood type. It's our blood. I run my hand along the rusted color, as if some of it will come off.

Cars start to honk at me. "Get out of the road!" one driver yells as he maneuvers around me. He's right. I'm crazy to be here. I run to the pedestrian walkway before someone hits me.

I sit on the cold concrete bench, leaning forward with my hands folded in front of me. *Oh, Grace*, I think. *It should have been me, or at the very least I should be with you.* Why do I get to live? There's this overwhelming pressure for my life to mean something. I must have been spared for a reason, right? What if I don't live up to the expectations? What if I fail in my choices and my life is some regular, boring life?

My leg shakes. Grace used to hate it when we were younger and I sat behind her in class and put my foot on her chair and bounced it. She'd say she was experiencing her own personal earthquake. Grace usually insisted on being right and wouldn't budge until you gave. She was very practical, a bottom-line thinker. I used to drive her crazy with not wanting to make a decision until the last minute. She was always planning. She was always humming. She could always make me laugh or talk sense into me. I think about how much I need her and how hard life has been without her.

I want Grace back. I want things to be the way they used to be. I want to know what I'm supposed to do now. I want someone else to figure it all out. I don't want to be left with some stupid to-do list. Four down, only one left to go. I thought there'd be some closure completing it, like if I did all the things on the list I wouldn't miss her so much.

But I still miss her. And the pain of her death hasn't left. It's not as raw as it used to be, but it's still deep, embedded like a dull knife. If only I could remove that blade, maybe the pain would lessen.

"I'm so sorry," I whisper.

The words repeat in my mind, but in a different voice. On the night of the accident, the other driver said he was sorry over and over. I remember the anguish in his eyes.

I wipe the tears from my face with the sleeve of my shirt. I can't keep coming back here. Grace isn't here; she never was. I head back to my car. Dad and Jenny will be worried, so I should go home. *I want to go home.* I get a text as I'm walking. It's Hanna.

Where are you?

Going home. You feeling okay?

Yeah. Sorry if I freaked you out

I've seen worse ha ha

Seriously, thank you

You're welcome

It was a beautiful sunrise though

Yeah

It was, until Hanna almost died. But she didn't. She didn't die. She will live and see another sunrise. And for the first time since the accident, I don't feel guilty about hoping I'm there with her.

Later that night I can't sleep. I get up to see if there's anything to eat. Light slips underneath the door to Grace's room. I hesitate, then knock softly.

"Come in," Dad says.

I find him sitting on the floor in his robe with a couple of Grace's notebooks spread out around him.

"Couldn't sleep?" he asks.

I shake my head.

"Me neither." He gestures to the books. "Grace was so talented. I knew she wrote, but she kept it close to her. I'm sorry if this upsets you, but after today, when I thought—when I got that call from the hospital . . . I needed to read them."

"No, I get it." I sit down next to him. "Can I see one?"

Dad hands me a small red journal. I open it to the first page. The date is two years ago, right at the start of the school year. I flip through the pages and laugh at her Top Five People to Avoid, but what surprises me is that River is number four. Was she trying to avoid him because he annoyed her or because she liked him? Probably the latter. Girls are always playing games like that, though it's hard for me to imagine Grace as one of those girls. She was pretty straightforward with me. But I was her brother, not a potential love interest.

Mark is such a jerk. Sometimes I hate him. But I love him too. I'll get him back when he's least expecting it.

I have no idea what she's referring to, but obviously it was something big. I don't fight the tears that come. After burying the hurt for so long, it's like a current I can't suppress anymore. I don't want to. I'm tired of running from it. "I've been so angry. I miss her so much."

"I miss her too. She was my daughter. It's unnatural and unthinkable to have to bury your own child. But you two—you shared a closeness that I can't imagine." His eyes fill with tears.

Sitting here, crying with my dad, feeling a little awkward, owning what I need to, I take it a step further.

"I'm sorry for not thinking about how hard it's been on everyone."

He puts his hand on my arm. "We'll get through this. We'll find a way, together."

He removes his hand and wipes his eyes.

"She say anything good in yours?" I point to the notebook he has open. Dad offers it to me, but I ask him to read it out loud instead.

He puts his glasses back on.

I know God has a purpose for my life. It doesn't have to involve saving the world or anything, but I want my life to matter.

That makes my heart ache a little. Grace died before she ever got to discover her purpose, though I suppose her living and us knowing her was already a big win for us. She changed all of us, and still does even now that she's gone.

Dad reads another.

There's enough suckage to go around the world like fifty million times. I'm going to start a national campaign. We need a day where people unite and not suck together. I'll call it "The day where everyone agrees not to suck."

I laugh because hearing Dad say the word "suck" so much is really funny.

We take turns reading passages from Grace's journals. At some point, Jenny notices Dad isn't in bed and comes in. She sits on the floor next to Dad and me. She joins us reading Grace's words. There is laughter and tears. Grace's voice is loud and clear on the page and spreads across the room like a healing salve. Fern even wakes and comes in and sits on my lap. Even though there are only four of us in the room, she is here. Grace is here. We are a family again.

Twenty-Eight

sit inside my car across the street from the house. I'm working up my courage. Grace thought I didn't ever fear anything, but that's not true. I just hide it better than most. But today isn't about Grace. Today is about me choosing life. I take a deep breath and let it out in one big whoosh before exiting the car. I check myself in the window. I've removed my beanie, and smooth my hair with my hands. I'm wearing a button-down black shirt, my nicest pair of jeans. I'm ready.

I knock on the brown door. A few moments later a woman answers.

"Hello, Mrs. McAllister? My name is Mark Santos. I was wondering if Mr. McAllister is here."

Her eyes widen as she recognizes my name, but she says, "Yes, let me get him."

She closes the door partly and doesn't invite me inside. Cautious. Who knows what she's thinking. Maybe I scare her. Does she think I'm here for revenge? I'd probably think the same thing.

Mr. McAllister comes to the door wearing jeans and a T-shirt. I wouldn't have known him because my memory of him is more like an outline.

"Mr. McAllister, my name is Mark Santos."

"Yes, yes, Mark." His voice is how I remembered. "Come in," he says, and I follow him inside to the kitchen table.

"Can I get you anything? Some water? Orange juice?"

"Water is fine," I say because my throat is suddenly dry.

The TV is on in the living room, playing a cartoon I like. The backs of two kids' heads remind me of how Grace and I used to do the same thing on Saturday mornings. He places two waters on the table. I reach out and take a drink, trying not to shake the glass.

"Mr. McAllister."

"Tony, you can call me Tony."

"Tony." I clear my throat. "I came here—well, this isn't the first time I've come. I haven't known what to say, so I usually drive off."

297

He pales a little at my admission. He's probably thinking that I'll hurt him, and honestly there's a small part of me that would like to break this table and go to town on his face. But I don't.

"After Grace's death, I wanted you to die. I wanted you to suffer. But then I came here and saw you playing out front with your kids. And . . . it didn't make sense to wish that anymore."

I take another sip of water. His wife watches me from a spot inside the kitchen. Her hands grip the side of a counter as if she's afraid.

"What I'm trying to say is, I know it was an accident. What happened will never really make sense. I'd give anything to have Grace back, but that's not possible. I have to keep moving forward or I'm not really living, and Grace wouldn't want that for me. She wants . . . She'd want me to live. So part of my doing that is telling you . . . I forgive you."

When I say the words, Tony stares down at the table and puts his head in his hands. He starts to cry, and not a stoic-man cry, but a big-sobs kind of cry. His wife comes and wraps her arms around him. There are tears in her eyes. The only reason I'm not crying too is because I'm pretty much cried out for a while. But I tell you, it feels good to see him cry. Not because I've hurt him. I can tell there's no torture I could inflict that he hasn't done to himself. He'll have to live with Grace's death the

Twenty-Nine

avoid Hanna after she comes home from the hospital. Seeing her almost lose consciousness and leave in the back of the ambulance freaked me out. I still get choked up thinking about it. We need to talk, but I'm like a liter of soda that's been shaken a hundred times and is ready to blow. I'm just trying to get a handle on all the emotion.

I know I'm being stupid, and she'll probably be all worked up about why I haven't made any effort. We're both on winter break, so she knows I'm around. We've also got the 5K soon. I need to make the first move here. The longer we go without speaking, the more awkward it gets. I should text her, let her know I'm thinking about her.

I text Sebastian instead.

rest of his life. I feel good because I know that my forgiveness is part of what he needs to heal. It also gives me hope that one day I'll be able to fully forgive myself.

He reaches across the table to shake my hand. I take it. His grip is strong and I try to match it.

"Thank you," he says. "You didn't have to come. I can only imagine what courage it has taken you. Your forgiveness makes the load a little more bearable."

One of the boys watching the TV says, "Daddy, what's wrong?" He comes over and looks at me. "Who are you?"

"He's a friend of your dad's," Tony's wife says.

"But why are you crying?"

"Daddy's just happy," Tony says.

I smile at the kid and stand to leave. My last glimpse is of the three of them sitting at the table in a group hug. I let myself out and head for my car.

My phone buzzes.

Today it's how she'd make animal shapes out of pancakes.

Lily. Her texts come at random, but I like them. They make it okay to remember.

I respond.

Today it's how we used to fight over Saturday morning cartoons.

Where are you?

Los Feliz

Coming over

Right on

The smell of Korean BBQ hits me as soon as I enter the small parking lot. I never get tired of that smell. I've timed my visit with lunch, so there's a long line of people. Sebastian sees me through the truck window and motions for me to come around.

I walk to the back of the truck where Sebastian opens the door and hands me a white apron and hairnet.

"Come on. I need help. Alex is sick."

"I'm not wearing that." I point to the hairnet, but I grab the apron and tie it around my middle.

"Yes, you are. Just think of it as a beanie with air-conditioning," he says.

I put on the hairnet and follow him. If you ever think the inside of one of those food trucks looks bigger than it does on the outside, you'd be wrong. It's cramped and tight, especially depending on how many people you have in there. We have three: Sebastian; his older brother, Eddie; and me. Eddie tells me to get a number two plate ready.

I look at Sebastian for help and he points to the hanging menu. "Like you don't have it memorized already."

A number two is four short ribs, rice, kimchee, and a drink. I pile it on the plate the way I remember Sebastian handing it to me. Sebastian gives me the thumbs-up as he passes it to the customer through the window. Next up is a burrito. Eddie shows me how to make one with beef, kimchee, fried rice, cheese, lettuce, salsa, and hot sauce. He wraps it up in two seconds and returns to cooking. He's back and forth stirring, flipping, and mixing. He's a machine.

It only takes ten minutes for them to get me off the food line because I'm too slow, so they put me in charge of taking orders and money. This I can handle. I've been a cashier at Dad's stores, so I know how to work a register. It's even easier in the truck because they only take cash, no credit cards. Pretty soon we have a good rhythm going. Two hours pass quickly and the bulk of the lunch customers have all been served.

Sebastian and I get a small reprieve and head outside for some air. Eddie stays in the truck and takes a call on his phone.

"That was intense," I say, and take a drink of water.

"You did good. A natural. Maybe you should think about going into food service," Sebastian says.

I stretch my neck. "Not for me. That's harder than I thought." And I'm not into the uniform. We're both still wearing the aprons, now stained with food, and hairnets.

"When it's busy. When we're not, it's boring and hot being in the truck all day."

"You planning on joining the family business?"

"They'd like me to. Look." He takes out an envelope stuffed in his back pocket. "I meant to show you earlier."

It's an early acceptance letter from UCLA. "Dude, that's awesome." I high-five him.

"I'll probably work with the truck, since I'm going to stay local."

"So it's been decided?" I toss my water bottle into a nearby trash can.

"That's why I applied for early admission." Sebastian takes out a hacky sack and tosses it to me with his feet. "What about you?"

"Berklee's due in a couple of weeks," I say, and flip the sack into the air and catch it with my toe before sending it back to him.

"Boston. Not too far from LA."

"No, not too far. You could drive the truck. I bet Korean BBQ would be a hit."

"It's already there."

I take off my apron because I'm not used to playing hacky sack with a skirt on. We keep talking while bouncing and tossing the sack around, something we've been doing since freshman year. Sebastian is better than me. I've always told him it's because he's closer to the ground.

"You going to apply?" he asks me.

"Yeah," I say. I've started thinking about the future again, about how I don't want to waste a year trying to figure things out. I can go to school without knowing the whole plan. "I'm going to send it in after I make an audition video."

"Nothing to worry about there. You were born to play the bass."

"Yeah, I'm pretty good," I say, and laugh. I can't imagine anything else I'd rather do than make music.

"How's Hanna?" Sebastian asks.

I drop the sack. "Good, I think." I pick it back up with my foot and bounce it a few times to get the rhythm again before tossing it to Sebastian.

"I wish I'd been there to help."

"Yeah. I could have used it. I think I pulled something carrying her." I chuckle. It's my attempt to joke about it.

"You going to call her?" he asks.

"Maybe, why?"

"She may have asked me about you when we talked yesterday."

"So you're the new guy best friend?"

He grunts. "She thinks you're avoiding her. Look, just call her, so I don't have to be in the middle. I don't do the whole guy-best-friend thing. She talked for thirty minutes. I can't keep that up."

"I'm going to call her." I am. I will. I don't know what to say, but I need to face her, or rather, face my feelings. The perfect situation comes to mind. "In fact, I'm going to see if she wants to go bowling."

"Since when do you bowl?"

"Everyone bowls."

"Want to practice with Charlie later?"

"Can't tonight. I have another practice." Since Hanna pulled through, I figured I should do one of the things I had bargained with God as I carried her down the mountain. I e-mailed Marty and told him I could play bass again at church when he needed me. He needed me that week.

Eddie sticks his head out of the door of the truck. "Break's over," he calls.

Sebastian pockets the sack and I tie the apron back on.

"Ready," we say, and head for the truck.

"So when did you start bowling?" Hanna asks as we pull into the bowling alley two nights later.

"I picked it up recently."

"When you asked if I wanted to hang out tonight, I wasn't expecting this. I'm not really dressed for bowling." Her fingers play with the edge of her jean skirt.

"You look good to me. What were you expecting?"

She shrugs. "Hanging out at your house or maybe a trip to the bridge."

"My bridge days are over," I say.

"Really?" She doesn't sound like she believes me.

"Come on," I say.

I lead her inside and over to the Chinese restaurant. The group is sitting in the same spot in the back. A couple of the women see me and wave me over. Hanna's eyes shoot me questions as I introduce her, though she's already met some of the group from the candlelight service.

Greg and I shake hands. We sit and he begins the meeting. It's similar to the last time, with people taking turns sharing about their twin or about how they're dealing with their loss. When it comes to me, I tell them about how I went and forgave Tony.

"How do you feel now?" Greg asks.

"It's hard to put in words. Relieved, I guess. A part of me still hates the guy, but I think that's okay. Maybe one day I won't even feel that anymore. It feels good to do something to make Grace proud again." I feel Hanna's eyes on me, but I don't face her.

"Thank you for sharing that with us, Mark," Greg says.

He guides the discussion to business items, and then we are all set to bowl. This time I at least know how to pick out a ball.

On my first turn, I follow the three steps that Ann taught me last time. The ball heads straight down the aisle toward that sweet spot between the first and the second pin. I wait at the line, watching the ball, hoping I'll get a strike.

"Ooh, you got it, Mark," Ann calls out behind me.

I believe her. This is it. The strike's gonna happen. In the last second, the ball wavers and hits only four pins. I turn around and throw both arms up in the air as if to say, *I'm awesome*.

My team applauds and high-fives me.

"You're getting the hang of it," Jessica says.

"Yeah, you've been practicing," Greg says, and laughs.

Because of our numbers, Hanna's actually on the competing team. She gets up and, even in a little jean skirt, bowls a strike with a professional-looking curve ball. She turns and offers a smug grin.

"Hey!" I say as she sits down next to me. "Not bad."

"Junior high bowling team," she says.

"I forgot about that."

"Come on, Mark, rub the ball," Ann says. I reach out and give the ball she's holding a good massage. "We need all the help we can get, with you giving a ringer to the other team." She winks at me before stepping up. She bowls a strike and does a little dance.

"She's hilarious," Hanna says.

"Yeah."

"It's good to see you so happy."

The word would have made me cringe a couple of months ago, because it seems so shallow, so easy to fake. I also couldn't imagine myself ever happy without Grace. I had resigned myself to thinking I didn't deserve to be happy ever again.

"I'm on my way to happy," I tell her, which is the truth.

"On your way to happy," she says. "I'll take that."

I'm up again. "Wish me luck."

"Luck."

This time I don't concentrate as much. I walk slowly to the line and let the ball go. Gutter ball. I still get high fives and whistles from my team.

We don't speak on the drive home. It's not an uncomfortable silence, more of a quiet between two people who don't have to prove anything to each other. But there's something else in the silence, something that's been between us for years, which I've tried to ignore or avoid. But I'm tired of avoiding. I park, and Hanna's about to say good-bye when I ask her, "You tired?"

"Not really."

"Come on, let's take a walk."

"I can't believe it's Christmas in four days," she says as we make our way up the street. "Senior year is going too fast. Everything is happening too fast."

"Get all your shopping in?" I ask her.

"Yeah."

"Did you get me anything?"

"We're buying each other gifts now?" she asks, turning toward me with a playful grin.

"Maybe."

"Well, don't hold your breath. I don't know if I'll have time."

We walk side by side. The sky is dark except for a few tiny stars. The moon is nowhere to speak of. With each step I'm working up the courage. How many times have we done this? Walked our streets. Her body fitting perfectly alongside mine. Talking about nothing that turns into something that becomes nothing again.

"Steve's moving in January twentieth," she says. "They took me out to dinner to discuss it, so I'd be involved in the process. It's not bad. He's not bad. It's change, you know. And that can be a good thing."

I decide now's the time to either go big or go home. I take her hand. We continue walking as if it's the most natural thing for us to be holding hands. I want to say something, to define this moment, but I can't find the words.

I think of the line from Grace's poem, *Lots of things can happen between seventeen and forever.* It's true. I don't know if it'll work out, if we'll be together ten years from now or even next year. I only know that her hand is warm in mine. I know that I want Hanna.

"When we were on that mountain, when you looked like ..." I have to stop speaking at the thought of Hanna slumped over, barely responsive.

"I was so stupid," Hanna interrupts in a rush of words.

309

"Careless. I didn't anticipate how strenuous the hike would be. I didn't want to have to carry anything up there, so I left my bag in the car. I forgot I had silenced Pepe's alerts the night before. It was like all the worst things that could happen actually happened. The doctor told me if it wasn't for you, I could have gone into a coma or even died. You saved me."

I let that sink in. *I saved her.* I couldn't save Grace, but I saved Hanna. In a way, she also saved me. She stuck by me, even when I was messed up. She's still here with me.

"We're like this cliché," I say. "The boy and the girl across the street."

"It'll never work," she says softly.

"Probably not." I stop and face her. She looks up at me. I reach out and touch her hair. It's soft, like I knew it would be. "But here's the thing: You're my Top Five."

She smiles big. "Which number?"

"The whole thing."

I lean forward and kiss her. Her lips are soft and cool because of the night air. It's better than I imagined. My whole body trembles, so I cup her face with my hands, but it's not enough. I wrap my arms around her, drawing her body close to mine, and kiss her. Hanna's hands circle my neck and pull me in, and I feel like I'm going under, so I anchor myself to her as the deep sea of night swirls around us.

Thirty

The weatherman had predicted rain, but there's not a gray cloud in the sky. In fact, there aren't any clouds. It's a perfect blue.

Have a great run. It's a text from Mom. I have to admit, I still get a little thrown when I see it's her. I'm not totally comfortable, but I'm trying, and I think that's what's important.

Thanks.

See you in a couple of weeks?

Roger that

I don't know if Mom and I will ever be superclose, but I'm giving her what she wanted. I'm giving her a chance. Which is all that anyone is really asking for.

My family and Hanna check in. It's a relatively smooth

process. We're all given a number that we pin to our chests. Even Fern gets a number. My parents are going to walk the route with her.

I find Sebastian stretching in the grass near the starting line. I'm surprised to see Pete with him; I didn't know he signed up. I'm not surprised that Pete looks like a runner from the '80s, with his blue sweatband, white T-shirt that says I HEART RUNNING, and blue shorts.

"That's a serious outfit," I say. "I didn't know you ran."

"I'm a man of many talents."

"I have a headband too," Fern says, and points to the purple band holding back her hair.

"We can be running partners," Pete tells her.

We join them stretching and make a wider circle.

"The famous Hanna," Pete says. "Nice to finally meet you."

She raises an eyebrow at me but says, "Likewise. Oh, and congrats on the Otis thing. Mark told me." After the show, Pete was granted early acceptance.

"Thank you."

"That looks like River," my dad says, gesturing to a tall guy in the registration line.

"Yeah, I told him about it. River!" I yell.

He jogs over to us after checking in, the only real runner of our group. My dad and Jenny give him a hug.

"Glad you could make it," I tell him as he plops down next to Hanna. She also gives River a hug. It's an emotional, huggy day, I guess. I give him a head nod. It's the closest thing he'll get to a hug from me. I haven't completely changed.

"Maybe you should say something?" Hanna whispers.

"Thanks for coming, everyone," I say all formally. "This is the last—actually, it was number one on Grace's Top Five. It's crazy that we actually did everything before the year ended, just like she wanted. Or maybe it wasn't what she really wanted, but it's what we needed. We miss you, Grace. See you at the finish line."

An announcer tells us to begin lining up at the starting line. Since we aren't really competing, we aren't positioned at the front with the serious runners. We're all kind of somewhere in the middle. Dad and Jenny stand on either side of Fern, holding her hands. Sebastian and Pete are on the other side of me. Sebastian sets his watch.

"Okay, I figure it'll take me thirty minutes, though I'm not in running shape. It's only a 5k. A little over three miles. No problem." He swings his arms back and forth, as if to psych himself up.

"It's not a competition," I tell him.

"Everything's a competition. I can at least take Pete."

"Keep talking," Pete says. He pulls up his long white-and-blue-striped socks.

River jumps up and down and shakes out his head and his

arms. I wonder if I should do the same thing. If that's what you're supposed to do to warm up or something.

Hanna takes my hand and squeezes it, distracting me from River. I kiss the top of her head, but she takes my face and pulls me in for a quick kiss. I thought my parents might be a little freaked about Hanna and I taking our friendship to another level, but all Jenny said was, "It's about time," followed by, "Don't blow it."

I don't plan on it.

"On your mark," the announcer, standing on top of a ladder, says into a microphone. The whole group gets into a running stance and freezes. "Get set. Go." He fires a gun.

We surge together like a cresting wave. It takes only a couple of paces for us to separate, with River taking off ahead. My family is somewhere in the back. I've told Hanna I'll stay with her. I can't see Sebastian and Pete, so I don't know if they're in front or behind us. It doesn't matter where they are. I know they're all running with me. It's where they've been all along, right by my side for when I needed them, even when I tried to push everyone away.

I picture Grace running too. She's smiling with her black hair in a high ponytail swinging and bouncing as she runs. She would have loved this: all of us together, united by our love for her.

I match my pace with Hanna's, but she tells me, "Go."

"You sure?"

"Yes." She laughs. "Go," she says again.

I open my stride, and with each step, I think about how good it feels to run.

Acknowledgments

Thank you so much to everyone who made this novel possible:

To Joshua Suaverdez, for being my original muse for Mark all those classes ago.

To the following friends for helping me out with the details: Samantha Duke for all her Pepe knowledge, Lovejoy Ontiveros for her insight and willingness to answer random texts at any time, Isabelle Logie for letting me follow her around school, Nate Lawler for his surfing lesson, Wayne Miller for his bass expertise, and Niko Embry for giving me a glimpse into the head of a bass player and future rock star.

To the baristas at Swork, who by now know my order before I even place it.

Thank you to Mom and Michelle for being early readers and for all your support and encouragement.

To Mosaic, my tribe of dreamers, always faith, hope, and love.

To my parents, who still think I'm awesome simply because I'm their daughter. To David and my kids, who are the best sojourners I could ask for.

Thank you to Annette Pollert for being excellent at what you do. You make everything better. Thanks also to the whole team at Simon Pulse.

Finally to Kerry Sparks, my wonderful agent: it starts with you.

I am deeply grateful to all.